THE OTHERS FROM R.M. GILMORE

DYLAN HART

The Scene
Endless Night
Sacrifice
Forsaken
Bound
White Walls

PRUDENCE PENDERHAUS

17 Marigold Lane
19 Marigold Lane
21 Marigold Lane

And the Creek Don't Rise

ENDLESS
NIGHT
Dylan Hart
SERIES
R.M. GILMORE

Anniversary Edition

Edited by Becky Johnson

Design by RMGraphX

978-1-7358635-5-9

Mac Gille Mhur Publishing

For Si-Obi-Wan.
I love your precious heart.

As I was going to St. Ives,
I met a man with seven wives,
Each wife had seven sacks,
Each sack had seven cats,
Each cat had seven kits:
Kits, cats, sacks, and wives,
How many were there going to St. Ives?

-Unknown, *1730*

ONE

IT WAS ALWAYS AWKWARD BEING IN MIKE'S HOUSE. Standing in his living room, looking at pictures of us hanging on every wall, standing framed on every surface. It was weird to think he walked around in that house every day with my face staring at him from all angles. I always wondered why he never took them down. I'd hung most of them there when we moved in and I left them right where they hung the day I walked out. Apparently, so had he.

"You never know," Mike said from the bathroom.

I looked in the direction of his voice to see a sliver of light around the doorjamb; he hadn't bothered closing the door. It felt all too natural talking to him through a crack in the bathroom door. Like nothing had ever changed. I leaned against the edge of the couch just down the hall from the bathroom and listened to the water running in the shower.

"Never know what?" I asked, loud enough he could hear me over the running water.

Small wafts of steam puffed out from the opening in the door, and with it, the smell of his soap. I hadn't had the pleasure of that smell in a long time. I closed my eyes and breathed in deep.

"The truth," he replied, just after he turned the water off.

I could hear him moving around the small room. Clanking his toothbrush in the cup, opening and closing the medicine cabinet, all the little mundane tasks we took for granted every day. Those little sounds of daily life pulled me back into a time I thought I'd almost forgotten. A time I was in love. A time I was safe and happy. A time I could never get back.

"And you do? Does anyone ever really know what's real?" I questioned, looking at a picture of the two of us that hung on the wall only inches from my head. We looked so happy. Wide smiling faces and bright eyes.

"Not usually, no. But you could, if you wanted to." His voice came clearer than it had before. I glanced away from our shining faces to see Mike had emerged from the bathroom, shower wet and towel clad.

He never met my eyes when he turned from the bathroom and walked away from me. The deep indent that trailed from between his shoulder blades to the small of his back shifted and moved with every step. I hadn't forgotten what his body looked like, I just hadn't thought about it in a while. An unconscious smirk and tweak of my brow came with the memory of every moment I'd laid eyes on the better half of that man. Mike cleared the space between the bathroom and his bedroom door wearing only a small, stark white towel around his waist. He seemed to not care that I was in perfect eyeshot of his half-naked body. Part of me was content with the situation. Then there was a part of me, the logical part, which said there was no way in hell *it* was ever going to happen. I happily ignored that part and enjoyed the view.

A few steps before he reached the privacy of his room, he pulled the towel from around his waist and brought it up to dry his wet hair. In that tiny second, I caught a glimpse of the backside I'd been missing for damn near two years. Two dimples sat just above his nicely rounded cheeks and just below the curve of his back. My throat made a small noise before I caught it and moved on. The sight of something so long missed can wreak havoc on your psyche, and that was the last damn thing I needed.

"What is it that you want?" I asked. I wasn't sure where he was going with the conversation. And seeing all that he had to offer, well, not *all*, but a lot, made me forget why I was standing in his living room in the first place.

"The same thing you do." He came out of his room and walked down the hall toward me; his wet hair messy from the towel. He'd put on pants. Just pants.

Mike stopped a few feet from me. I could still smell his soap. I tried hard not to look at the expanse of his chest and shoulders. He wasn't a chiseled masterpiece, not even close. But he had the look of someone who could scoop you up in his arms and carry you to safety. Not that he'd ever tried to pick up my fat ass. I tried to look him straight in the face as I had always been able to do, but all I could think about were those two little divots just above his ass. My eyes jerked away to move down his body and caught an eyeful of the pale line of hair that led from the top of his jeans to his belly button.

Holy shit.

My breath caught in my throat, but I managed to squeak out, "What is it you think I want?" I decided looking at his face was probably the best idea.

He smiled and stepped closer. I liked his smile. It made his eyes crinkle on the sides. Standing that close to Mike felt as natural as putting my shoes on, but I knew it wasn't right. I knew there was no way it was a good thing. He was acting like nothing had changed. Like we were still… us.

"What's wrong, babe?" His brows pulled together in the center, looking down at me from his six-foot-whatever stature.

I just shook my head. I had no idea what to say. He'd never put me in that position before. Not in a long time had he been so… naked. I'd thought for a long time it was completely over. That I was done with it. With us. I'd come to terms with it and moved on. My tenacity was the only reason we were able to stay as some sort of friends.

An expression passed over his face I hadn't seen in a long time. His eyes saw straight into me and dug around inside. Like he was planning every moment with me from then on out. Like he'd never leave me. He'd die for me.

The muscles in his chest flexed and his hand came up to wrap around the base of my neck. My heart literally stopped beating. I watched his face, looking for some kind of motive. Waiting for the truth to rear its ugly head.

"When you run, I'm here," he promised, as if it wasn't a seriously weird thing to say. "Believe in nothing you can't reach out and touch."

Out of sheer compulsion, I reached out and touched his chest. He was warm and solid.

"I love you, Dylan Hart." His mouth said those words without hesitation, without an ounce of regret. He crooked his head and leaned down toward me. The smell of his soap so strong I thought I'd climbed inside of him. Drops of water fell from his wet hair onto my face and trickled down my cheek like tears. Maybe they were. I didn't care. I waited, ready, for him to kiss me. Wanting to remember so terribly what those kisses felt like and waiting for him to remind me.

The heat from his breath tickled my lips. With heavy breaths, my heart pounded in my chest. I lifted myself up onto my tiptoes, forcing my lips to meet his.

BAM-BAM-BAM

My body lurched and jerked and tumbled from the couch to the floor. "You've got to be fucking kidding me!" I yelled loud enough for the neighbors to hear.

I laid there for a moment on my plush carpet trying to get a grip on reality. After a few deep breaths, truth flooded into my head, and I knew where I was. I was at home, lying on my living room floor, desperately wishing the last fifteen minutes of my life had been reality.

The twinge of impure thoughts hit my stomach as I recalled the image of Mike and I knew it was wrong. My psyche had taken me on a journey into the past, and it was fun while it lasted, but that shit was long gone and it was never coming back. Not if I had anything to do with it anyway.

Yeah, right, okay.

My bags had been packed and I'd been waiting—or sleeping—on the couch for three hours when the cock block du jour knocked on the door and took me away from potentially the first piece of ass I'd gotten in over a year. Subconscious or not, it was still more than I'd had in a while. If left unchecked, sexual frustration apparently ran rampant in your dreams too .

I climbed up from the floor, wiped the residual drool from my cheek, and stomped toward the door.

"Fuck, Tatum, take you long enough?" I said in a huff as I flung open the front door.

"I'm sorry. I just couldn't decide on what to wear." I stood in shock in the open doorway. My eyes locked on to the beautiful white smile that was plastered on the man standing on my porch. "Looks like you've had some trouble finding a hair brush this morning," he remarked, smoothing the side of my hair down and back into my ponytail while I stood there with my mouth agape.

"Cyrus. What are you doing here?" I grilled, flabbergasted. His perfect form nearly filled the doorway. It had been almost five months since I'd laid eyes on him. I would swear he'd gotten prettier in that time. It didn't help I'd been knee deep in butt dimples just a few minutes before opening the door to this beautiful, yet entirely unwanted, surprise.

"Our lovely Tatum has taken too long to ready herself, so I have been asked to escort you to the airport." Brows pulled together, I questioned his existence with my glare. "Is that a problem for you?" he asked seriously, voice seeming almost hurt. His smile faded and a look of sadness moved across his perfect golden brown face.

Rhetorically I asked, "Do I have a choice?", and turned to move into the living room and retrieve my canvas messenger bag plus one large rolling suitcase.

"You could drive yourself," he spoke through an obvious snicker from his place in the doorway.

I let out a scoff that nearly shot a bit of snot from my nose. Luckily, my back was turned so wiping it away proved to be stealthy. Cyrus stayed in the doorway, watching my every move.

I was annoyed that Tatum hadn't come to get me. She was the only reason I was getting on that torpedo of death headed to the Big Easy to rub elbows with a horde of bloodsucking fiends. She promised we'd hang together and have a blast. She'd told me how bored she'd be if she was stuck alone with Malcolm at his head honcho vampire meetings and begged me to come with her to keep her company.

Granted, the idea of snooping and getting an inside look at the world of vampires, no matter how fictitious they truly were, called to my inner curious cat. Four months of working on my fiction novel and I had nothing that wasn't already done to death. I was mere weeks away from becoming a dull boy .

I needed something raw, something fresh, and a trip to New Orleans to hobnob with the underground vampire elite was just what the voodoo doctor ordered.

Tatum and I had planned to meet Malcolm and Cyrus at the airport an hour before Cyrus knocked on my door. That left me to make the trip to LAX alone riding bitch in Cyrus' white SUV. I was not happy about the new arrangement. It wasn't that I hated him, because I didn't. In fact, I actually really liked him. That was the problem. It was too hard to focus when I was near Cyrus. Not to mention, half the time he was either driving me insane or causing me to question his motives. I'd just as soon have left him to be pretty somewhere other than in my living room.

Either he needed to be less attractive or I needed to get over my self-conscious bullshit.

Maybe I could maul his pretty face a bit. Bring him down a peg.

"I'll be just a minute," I called from the bedroom. It was a shock to the reproductive system seeing Cyrus only minutes after having a dreamy close encounter with Mike. Cyrus was pretty, but... he would never be Mike.

Cyrus waited patiently as I fixed my bed head and put my shoes on. I grabbed my house keys from their normal spot on my nightstand and ran my fingertips over the cold metal of my new best friend that sat beside them. The one and only thing that had allowed me to get a good night's sleep in the most recent months. After offing those two vampy boys in a basement full of blood, I'd become a bit hardened to society. Sleep was a fickle bitch when your mental images were a slideshow of blood, makeshift stakes, and decapitation. My gun let my off-kilter brain pretend it was safe long enough to catch some Z's. Unfortunately, I couldn't take a gun through the airport. Probably a good thing for Cyrus though. I snatched my phone from the charger on the wall, rolled up the cord, and grabbed a thick book just in case. Even if I didn't get time to read it, at least I could whack someone pretty good with the hefty hardback. Maybe it'd be Cyrus. I smiled to myself at the thought.

Getting twitterpated over a stupid boy made me want to throat punch myself. Let alone two stupid boys at once. Although, in the long run, Cyrus was the less complicated of the two. Surprisingly.

"I'm ready," I said as I walked through the living room, bags in hand.

I tried my damnedest not to meet his stark green eyes. The lustful hold he had on me had faded since the shooting incident. Apparently putting a bullet through someone you were fighting to despise helped the cause. Or it could have been the five months we'd spent not speaking. I still wanted to strip him down and screw him six ways 'til Sunday. But the unadulterated need to do as he wished had all but disappeared. Not looking into his perfect face was just a precaution. Especially considering my Mike dream had left me all kinds of lusty. Since I was almost a hundred percent sure Cyrus wasn't a cold-blooded killer, I could do as I pleased with him. I just preferred not to get any more involved than necessary with people who drank blood. Or their entourage.

Without a word, Cyrus pulled both my bags from my hands in one fell swoop and headed out the door with them. Not having to drag a suitcase and an overstuffed messenger bag down the stairs of doom was a blessing, but allowing him to take my stuff left me feeling like I owed him.

I stayed behind and made sure I'd shut everything off. We'd be gone three days which was absolutely long enough for my apartment to burn to ashes. Once satisfied I hadn't forgotten anything, I began the process of locking my damn door. As

visit them on their home turf would make anyone a bit jumpy. Even badass Dylan Hart. Did that mean I'd turn around and go home? Not on your fucking life.

And you wonder why you're always ass deep in alligators.

Once boarded, seated, buckled, and terrified, I pulled my phone out of the bigass bag I'd brought with me. I was shutting it off. I swear. I noticed I'd missed a call and a text from Mike. *Who else?* He hadn't left a message, just a quick text reminding me to be safe and have a fun trip. It was nice knowing someone besides the tall blonde I was on the plane with gave a shit about my well-being. Well, and besides my mom, but she doesn't really count. At the very same time, it was so fucking aggravating that he still couldn't let me go. Couldn't relinquish that control he always needed so badly to have over me. So says the woman who'd nearly hit a dreamland home run with those butt dimples of his. I let out a grumbling sigh and let my head fall back against the headrest.

"You're more likely to die in a car, they say," Cyrus said suddenly, breaking my miniature moment of solitude.

Without opening my eyes, I scoffed, "Humph, in a car I don't plummet to my death from forty-thousand feet."

"Plummeting would only occur should you drive yourself off a cliff I suppose...." He let his thought trail off.

That was not at all what I wanted to hear. "Don't give me the odds."

Giving up on relaxation of any kind, I let my eyelids slide open and took in my surroundings. Other would-be crash victims lugged their overstuffed bags and satchels through the aisle and passed my protruding elbow. Unlike the only other honest to goodness flight I'd been on, the bags didn't tear the shit out of my exposed skin. Thanks to the annoying red head, the four of us were flying first-class. Roomy seats, wider aisleways, and stiffer drinks. First-class was a far reach from the cesspool of sweaty asses crammed elbow to elbow in economy.

"Would you like to rest your head here…" He created an undue awkward pause before continuing, "…on my shoulder?" He was staring down at me when I dared to look in his direction.

Regardless of the roomy two-to-a-row seating in the snooty part of the plane, I was still too close for comfort to the sexiest man I'd ever been close enough to touch. It was going to be a damn long flight. I forced my eyes to look away as soon as I was able. It was only a matter of seconds, but I was left with the feeling I needed to look again. He had that kind of draw to him. If you didn't know he existed, you were fine. The second your eyes met his and he became real again, there was no going back. No one should ever be allowed to own a set of eyes so fucking pretty. It was downright dangerous.

The fasten seatbelt sign binged on and the few folks still standing promptly took their seats and buckled in tight. The captain came over the intercom with a pleasantly gruff voice greeting all his passengers, reminding everyone where the plane was headed, and thanking us for flying. The plane jolted to a start and rolled forward down the runway. We hadn't even left the tarmac yet, but my body knew where it was headed and it began protesting diligently. Out of sheer terror, I gripped the armrest and clenched my eyes tight. The sensation of leaving the safety of earth made my head spin and my breath nearly came to a full stop. I tried to breathe through the fear—in through the nose out through the mouth. Fuck that, it never worked. I was nearing a full-blown freak-out. The plane leveled itself and I tried to stay as quiet and nonchalant as I could, but my heart still tried to escape my body. An unexpected firm touch on my clenched hand brought me back to earth, so to speak.

"We're flying, you can open your eyes it won't kill you." Cyrus's sudden, soothing voice lulled my racing heart to a more controllable pace. I heard the seatbelt sign bing-off, and almost instantly people started rustling around.

At the suggestion of the idiot I should have never taken suggestions from, I opened my eyes. Tatum poked her head over the top of the seat in front of me. "You freakin' out yet, pussy?" she laughed, annoyingly smacking her gum. "Here, chew some gum, it helps." She handed me a little rectangle wrapped in shiny foil and returned to her seated position next to Malcolm.

I got the distinct feeling she'd be a little preoccupied during the flight. It also sank in that I was basically stuck next to the beautiful yet generally annoying Cyrus Atossa. Likely for the best part of my trip, in fact. I didn't know if it was my normal untrusting nature, or the fact that there was no way in hell the outward projection Cyrus put on was wholly honest, but I could not allow myself to fall ass over face for those sultry green eyes of his. Not to say I would've kicked him out of bed, but there was no way that would've been a lasting relationship.

He asked me a million and a half useless questions and I didn't want to be a total dick to the person I was stuck with for four hours, possibly days, so I answered them. I carried on a needless conversation with that beautiful man to keep my mind off the situation I found myself in. Besides, if the plane went down, he might be the last person I'd ever cling to for dear life. The last moments of your life should be pleasurable at the very least. Fortunately, it never came to that. Unfortunately, I'd made small talk with him for hours leaving nothing to talk about. Nothing but non-superficial, serious conversation. Of which I had no interest.

We landed at Louis Armstrong International just over four hours after the most terrifying experience of my life began. And I'd killed people. Not only was I forced to sit within touching distance of Cyrus, but the ride was less than pleasing. We hit a pocket of turbulence over some nondescript space of land about mid-way no more than ten minutes before the guy sitting two rows ahead of me upchucked all over his new bride. I nearly lost my cookies right along with him. If it weren't for the uncontrollable need to not utterly embarrass myself in front of the hunk sitting next to me, I probably would have.

Cyrus grabbed our carry-on bags out of the little cubby overhead and, at his insistence, kindly carried mine for me. I wasn't huge on chivalry, but I was even less attracted to carrying my own shit . He'd been all too happy to chauffeur my crap from one state to the next, and I was beginning to get suspicious. The four of us waited patiently for our luggage to come around the carousel. I'd half assumed someone like Malcolm McTavish would have a car waiting, a little servant boy dying to carry our things and cart us around at his beck and call. Someone other than Cyrus.

Cyrus hadn't come running to my aid at the baggage claim. My short legs and arms kept me too far on the peripheral of people waiting for their own shit to reach my bag. I stood there like a jackass while my biggest piece of luggage made its voyage right past me. Without thinking it through, I made the rash decision to chase it down rather than wait for it make its way around again. Dumb, completely fucking dumb. Without looking, I sidestepped to catch up with the ever-moving suitcase. My stubby fingers missed the floppy leather handle by a millimeter. Soft soled shoes shuffled softly to the right, trying to keep up. Still just out of reach, those two stupid feet of mine clumsily stepped over each other in a graceful effort to keep up with the moving belt carrying my livelihood farther and farther away. In one last desperate attempt, I lunged my upper half forward and reached my fingers as far as they would stretch. My left foot screeched its rubber sole across the linoleum flooring as my toe caught the floor and my chest landed uncomfortably against the metal edging of the carousel.

I'd caught myself before I fell flat on my face, but in the process, my frizzy brunette locks flipped over my face and became tangled in the oversized luggage tag of my fifty-pound suitcase. The suitcase continued its journey, dragging me head first along with it. Half-leaning over, my short little legs struggled to keep up. The soft white rubber of the soles on my Converse squeaked as they skidded across the linoleum floor. I could hear bystanders shuffling away from the idiot girl stuck to the roundabout. No one bothered to help. A little piece of me knew someone, somewhere, was filming the absurdities and I'd end up online. In a last-ditch effort, I used all my might to hoist the case from the moving belt and to the floor. The added weight caused my balance to shift. My valiant efforts were thwarted when the hefty case caused this Weeble to wobble and fall on her fat ass. Luckily, my hair freed itself in the commotion.

I stood as swift and catlike as I could manage, glancing around with cherry red cheeks. Hundreds of people hustled about doing their business as if nothing had happened. Well, mostly. A handful of gawkers stared, awestruck at my folly. Three of those gawkers were the three people I was depending on to watch my ass for the next few days.

Couldn't even hold a bitch's hair, what the fuck are you gonna do in a crisis?

Finally back on my feet, utterly embarrassed, and fully willing to slaughter the first person to crack some stupid joke, I had my shit and was ready to get the fuck out of Louis Armstrong International airport.

Malcolm hadn't hired a driver, but he had rented a pretty swanky car. Not a car person, I couldn't peg the make and model, but it was shiny and boasted a well-known emblem on the hood. The wide, leather back seat made for roomy ride. Also, I wasn't stuck driving. I was happy enough with that.

Our foursome piled onto the leather seats. No one even tried to look at me, let alone speak a word. I was fine with that. It was rare I took myself too seriously, but dammit, being dragged around by your hair from a luggage carousel while everyone watched crossed the line of funny into the realm of never-speak-of-this-again. Oh sure, after a few drinks it'd be funny and I could laugh it off, but until then, the world needed to leave me the fuck alone.

We drove in uncomfortable silence through an entirely unfamiliar city. I was pleased to just stare out the window. Cyrus breathed softly beside me, and I recalled the coolness of his breath I'd felt so close to my skin once at Embrace. The thought brought with it a chill and goose bumps down my arms. It'd been way too long since I had any kind of sex and it was taking its toll on my essence. I made a mental note to see what I could do to remedy that situation and moved on. No need to dwell on

"I could say the same about you and your… comrade," Cyrus responded, with an appropriately irritated undertone. My comrade was being a giant cunt. I didn't have much room to for shit talking.

"This new bullshit attitude she's adopted came along with the fiery ginger you call a boss. Or should I say *master*?" I snarled my lip in disgust and slammed the trunk shut.

I didn't really have a reason to have been so defensive about Tatum. She was a bitch, she knew it, I knew it, and she was fucking good at it, but God forbid anyone else called her out on it. Obviously, I had grown fond of the Amazonian hell bitch I called a friend. After twenty some-odd-years together, you kind of stopped noticing the bullshit and focused more on whose turn it was to be a dick. That was how we made it work anyway.

Cyrus lugged the larger bags ahead of me, up the begonia lined southern walk to the intimidating gray building. Great pillars supported a full wraparound balcony complete with wrought iron banisters and a couple of gargoyles perched to stand guard over the house of the undead. Nearly camouflaged with the cloudy sky, each layer of the house wore a different shade of gray. The house was itself a stormy sky, ominous and swollen with danger.

Large, drape-covered windows on the ground floor gave no evidence of the inhabitants and the smaller windows above were darkened to the point of near nonexistence. The houses on either side stood cheery in shades of yellow and blue, a stark contrast to that of the dreary erection.

Hee hee, erection.

Lugging suitcases and carry-ons, Cyrus and I made our way to the steps of the front porch. Tatum and her creep of a boyfriend waited, ever so patiently, for their *help* to arrive. Having about enough of their shit, I shoved the handle of Tatum's rolling case into her hand.

"Here," I said without a glance in her direction. Luckily for Malcolm, I hadn't carried any of his things; my shoving just might have gotten out of hand if I had something to shove and somewhere to shove it.

Malcolm gave a few raps on one side of the heavy double doors. A moment later, a rumble of thunder rolled through the air. I looked to the sky and caught a glimpse of a high attic window. No light shone through, but it intrigued me nonetheless. A high, darkened window, begging for the appearance of a singing butler to welcome us with ominous lyrics. What more could a little horror girl ask for in her lodgings for the weekend? One of the double doors opened and a peculiarly ambiguous being stepped into view. Tall and mostly lean muscle, the person teetered atop a pair of black patent leather platform boots. Miniature matching leather shorts and a strapless leather wraparound nipple cover were buckled from top to bottom with heavy silver buckles. It was one of the most ridiculous outfits I'd seen since I began the journey into the good, the bad and the bloody. With the weekend's itinerary still mostly a mystery, it likely wouldn't be the last.

Malcolm and Tatum slid through the door together and lingered in the doorway blocking the entrance for the rest of us lowly mules. I could hardly see around the giants, but I heard Malcolm making nice, introducing Tatum, and involving himself in some kind of mysterious greeting that involved lots of hand kissing and bowing. I let out an audible sigh at the ridiculousness of it all. Cyrus chuckled softly behind me. At least I wasn't alone out there on that gothic porch listening to the thunder roll in. After a few moments of hellos and howdy 'dos, the jackasses standing in the doorway moved enough to make way for us to move inside. Dragging luggage behind me, I noisily made my way past them all into the great entryway just inside the doors.

I stuck my hand toward the thing atop the humungous boots, "Pleasure to meet you Doctor Frank-n-Furter," I said with a wide grin. "Follow the bouncing thumb," I added, hand clenched in a fist, thumb bobbing around. No response. Not even a twinge in *its* eye.

Forever misunderstood.

I shrugged and turned from the freak show, meandering toward a sweeping archway to our right. Tatum caught me by the arm and said through her teeth, "What is your fucking problem?" I scrunched my face at her and wiggled my arm from her grasp.

Fuck that bitch.

I parked the rolling cases at the foot of a wide, rounding staircase and took advantage of my time alone while the vampires talked shop.

Or was it chomp?

Shut up.

My feet slid slowly across the marble floor, sneakers squeaking quietly against the tile floor. Hands shoved in my back pockets, I inspected my surroundings. Oversized, gold framed paintings hung sporadically around the high-ceilinged entryway depicting everything from an innocent young girl to the slaughter of a lamb on a sacrificial altar. The sight of all the red spilling over the edge of the painted slab made my shoulders tense. I remembered the gallons of blood that coated every inch of me after I'd crashed into buckets full of the red stuff. My mind flooded back to the images of the broken pool cue entering the soft flesh of a would-be vampire boy as I shoved it deep into his gut. I recalled the sight of poor Reggie and her missing head and the bloody stump just above her shoulders the killer had left behind when he, or she, snatched that head from her skinny body.

So many gory and horrifying images locked in my head, why am I not a fucking basket case?

You are, dumbass. You killed two vampire boys.

To save my life. Yet here I am, in the lion's den, ready to head out to party with a gaggle of blood drinkers.

Fucking certifiable.

More voices came into the room behind me. I turned to find three more of the welcoming committee greeting Malcolm and Tatum. It seemed Cyrus knew the drill and stood to the right and back a step from Big Red. I hated that bastard. I didn't even know why—alright, I had a few moderately valid reasons—but I could not stand Malcolm McTavish.

The three newbies kissed hands and cheeks and made their bows. Tatum followed suit, and it seemed to me like it wasn't her first rodeo, or blood bath, whatever. Of the three, one was female and the other two were male. The female looked so much like Dominika I had to look twice and stare really hard to make sure it wasn't, and even then I tuned in my ears to listen for the devilish accent before I was content it wasn't her. The two men, total opposites, reminded me of Laurel and Hardy. One was short, shorter than me, and so blond and white he might've been albino. He wore period garb down to the ruffled ascot and spats on his shoes. The other reminded me of Rasputin with his long black hair and piercing blue eyes. He stood a good foot taller than his buddy and even towered over Malcolm who stood a good foot taller than me. That was one big jar of redheaded mayonnaise, let me tell you.

Malcolm McTavish, Ronald McDonald's gigantic brother.

After a few moments of me ogling the haphazard gaggle of weirdoes, the tall one looked in my direction. It was the first time any of them noticed me since I'd attempted to introduce myself to the thing in the boots. Without a smile, a nod, any kind of acknowledgment, the tall guy stared at me with his intense eyes. Out of awkwardness, a little smile tugged at the corner of my mouth. Nothing. A few seconds passed, and I turned my body a bit to look behind me in the hopes maybe he was looking off at something I couldn't see. Nothing. I shoved my hands deeper in my pockets and looked back at the man. Still, he stared. Nervously, my eyes moved from his gaze. I raised curious brows and made a fart sound with my lips before I turned on my heel to walk away. Nowhere in particular, just anywhere but in the direct eye shot of that guy.

Hands still shoved in my pockets, I moved on, wandering mindlessly around the room. Everything you had ever seen in movies about modern vampires was wrong. There was nothing posh or chic in the general vicinity. Only furniture like Malcolm had at the office of *Sween,* his vampire quarterly magazine. Oversized claw-footed tables, Tiffany style lamps, and extravagant fainting couches.

These people are really into lounge chairs.

Off to the far left of the front door, a squared archway opened into a separate room. I think they called that room a parlor. A small sitting room with overly fancy furniture like my grandma had in her front room. Only, we were never allowed to sit on that furniture. Those assholes lazed on them like they were in an opium den.

All over the parlor, Victorian clad vampires lounged about chatting and mingling among themselves. No one noticed little ol' me peaking my head around the arched entryway. Dramatic rust--colored curtains cascaded from the ceiling and draped around the doorway. Each hooked with a loop to the inside wall.

I stood in awe at all the beautiful people lying about and made a bet with myself that not a one of them held down a normal job. Like the wake up with the sun and actually work kind. Most of them looked like they could be featured in Malcolm's magazine right along with Dominika and Cyrus. Perfect people make me want to punch infants.

I glanced over my shoulder toward the entrance where my so-called friends still stood like a group of walking, talking dildos. Malcolm continued some kind of ritual greeting with those that welcomed them into the home. Lots of unnecessary bowing, shaking and kissing if you asked me. I was more interested in what was going on in the room full of neat furniture and bloodsuckers.

I rolled my eyes and turned back to the scene of vampire people. All those perfect little bloodsuckers breathing perfectly good air and leaving little for the rest of us hacks. I hadn't even made it up the stairs and I was already regretting my decision to follow Tatum to New Orleans.

A couple sat adjacent from me, about fifteen feet away. The girl was young. If I had to guess, I'd say just this side of legal. The man she was cradled against looked as though he could be Cyrus's Viking brother. Sweeping stark blond hair fell over his well-structured pale face, brushing a set of equally blond brows. I'd been standing at the edge of the entrance to the parlor staring into the abyss of lazing Sanguinarians for well over three minutes and not one person, or whatever, noticed me. Until I took the chance to allow my gaze to linger on the blond version of Cyrus. I was innocently admiring his perfection when he caught my stare. A nasty snarl curled his powder-white face into an unattractive mess of skin and wrinkles. The sudden change to his expression sent a chill up my legs and into the back of my head before an aching in my stomach triggered my spidey sense. The once perfect specimen of Nordic manliness transformed into a grinning wraith. My breath caught and I took a step back. One of the loungers left his position near the curtains and pulled a thickly wound cord. The curtains closed with little effort, and the manic blond on the other side was out of sight.

Fear hit my heart and made it skip a beat. A fear I'd forgotten in recent months. A fear I'd learned to appreciate while hunting the killer of so many dead girls. A fear that told me to respect it or feel its wrath.

When I first stepped foot in Midnights Dream, I nearly exploded from holding in the laughter, but I later learned not all of those in the *scene* were horrendous losers offing hookers at every turn. In fact, some were stoic, some were beautiful, and some were fucking frightening. They may not explode in the sunlight or fear garlic, but immortal or not, one of them just might kill you where you stood.

Enter Deadly Bitch.

FOUR

AS SOON AS THE CURTAINS CLOSED, I WAS HURRIED OFF TO the farthest corner of the house. Malcolm didn't say much as he shuffled me up the stairs to what would be my room for the weekend. I worried that I was being taken to a darkened basement to be slaughtered and offered up to the vampire gods as a sacrifice. Malcolm led the way up the big curved staircase and along the landing on the second floor. We walked past at least two doors on the way, all closed. Of course, I snooped. It was what I did for a living. All chock full of curiosity. You know what they say about curiosity.

Yeah, I hate cats.

I'd lost Tatum on the first floor, but Cyrus stayed by Malcolm's side like a good little puppy. I was mostly thankful for that. I'd hate to see what would happen should Malcolm and I be left alone to our own devices.

Sadly, TSA had that pesky gun rule.

Dragging my rolling case behind me, I followed the fiery haired vampire boy to a second set of stairs. Cyrus had so kindly carried my messenger bag, but I wished he hadn't. All his chivalry was beginning to make me feel uncomfortable.

Fuck that, let the bastard carry your bags. What's it hurting aside from his masculinity?

Mine.

The second set of stairs was far less extravagant than the first and led to a mundane hallway much narrower than the second floor. I assumed it was once where they hid the help. I was just about to voice a formal complaint until I heard Malcolm tell Cyrus his room was just across the hall from mine. The ever-shrinking portion of my inner psyche that told me to stay away from Cyrus Atossa quickly became his biggest cheering section. The intense naughty thoughts that entered my head turned my face a cherry red and beaded with sweat.

Malcolm opened the door to my room, and I ducked in immediately, hiding my red face as best I could. The room was more expansive than I assumed it would be. It held an oversized, ornately decorated armoire and a four-poster bed complete with a chiffon canopy. Nothing I would have chosen for my bedroom at home, but definitely cool for a weekend in the den of Dracula.

I left my rolling case at the door and flopped down on my new bed. I could feel the familiar texture of a feather down comforter hidden under the pink and gold embroidered duvet. I took a quick count of pillows and came up with nine in total. I'd never seen that many pillows on a bed in my life. Tatum only had seven. I rolled onto my back and gazed up at the canopy. A matching shade of pink surrounded the four posts and draped from each all the way to the floor. A gaslight sconce provided the only light in the room but allowed me to see well enough to notice there was no outside light coming into the room. Thick maroon curtains hung to the floor on the wall opposite the door, but no sign of natural light peeked through.

"Where would you like your bag?" Cyrus asked cordially from the doorway.

"Anywhere is fine." I left my spot on the bed and headed toward the curtains in search of natural light.

My hands admired the velvet material of the drapes for a moment before I flung them back dramatically. No window. Instead, a mirror as tall as me adorned the wall.

"Who hides a mirror behind a curtain? Who has a room with no window?" I was mostly talking to myself. "Curiouser and curiouser," I said under my breath.

"This is only the beginning." I turned around and met the green eyes that stared a hole through me. He smiled and turned from me, leaving the room. Leaving me with only his ominous words.

"Do they rehearse this shit?" I thought aloud.

A monthly meeting of creepy bastards, perhaps. On the docket today, new ways to scare the shit out of people. Jesus.

I grabbed my smallest bag and pulled my phone from the side pocket. I figured I'd better call my mom; she wasn't overbearing or anything, only a normal mom with normal worries. Although, we hadn't talked much since my run-in with the law. I thought she was kind of in denial about the whole killing some people thing. It was the same selective denial she lived in when it came to Mike. One of the initial reasons we didn't talk much anymore. According to her, Mike and I were still going strong. All you needed was love she said.

She obviously smoked herself stupid in the seventies.

I turned my phone on after more than six hours of being off, and I had only one voice mail. I felt the love. I really did. My shoulders slumped a little as I listened to the message.

"Ba—Dylan, hey, it's me. Uh, Mike. Listen, we've got a situation churning out here I think you'd like to know about. Hey, uh, gimme a call back as soon as you get this." The line hung for a few seconds before the voice mail ended.

"Ugh, fuck." Reluctantly, I called Mike's number.

"This is Mike." I cringed. I hated when he answered like that.

Geez. "Hey, what's going on?"

"Hey. How's your trip?" said Mr. Nonchalant.

"Just getting started. And actually kinda shitty so far. You had some news for me?" I wasn't in the mood for Mike-shit.

"Yeah, you won't believe what's come across my desk."

"Wait," I said and closed my eyes, "if your next sentence has the words 'dead girl' in it, I'm hanging up." I was lying. I'd only ever legitimately hung up on him five times in all the years I'd known him and each time was well more deserving than dead girls.

"Okay. Um, well, you know Regina and the… one in Vegas," he paused.

"Yeah…." I clenched my teeth.

Fuck. Fuck. Fuck.

"There's more."

I leaned forward, resting my elbows on my knees. "More? How many?"

"Lots."

"Define *lots*," I demanded.

"Eight."

"Eight? In your jurisdiction?" The pitch of my voice peeked at an awkward level. Saying I was shocked would've been an understatement.

"No. Regina, Vegas, and six others. One just popped up in Texas three days ago. Same as Regina. Young, severed head, wooden object protruding from her chest, probable ties to the underground vampire community." It sounded like he was reading off a teleprompter. It was probably his handy dandy notebook.

How in the fuck do eight staked and headless bitches just fall under the radar? Why hasn't this hit the front pages yet? First vampires stalking the streets of Hollywood, now vampire hunters?

In every generation there is one....

"When did the others come up? Regina was killed five months ago, how long have these other precincts been holding out?" My head swam in death, but I regained composure by reminding myself at least I still had a head to swim.

Big tough Dylan Hart. Sleeps with her gun. Has no friends. Yup, that's me.

"Apparently, they've been turning up all over the country since March. Dylan, Regina wasn't the first. In fact, she was the third." His voice was dramatic and I got the feeling he was aiming for a shock and awe reaction on my end.

"Fuck." My heart sank a bit. I always assumed her death had something to do with Diego and Sam and the bloody mess they'd all gotten into. I knew there was a similar case in Las Vegas a few months later, but I figured it was some attempt to copy the original. "So, what are you doing about it?"

"I'm gonna need to talk to your friends. They've got to have an idea about what's going on. I wouldn't doubt they knew about all these murders and haven't said a word. Shit, maybe it's some kind of punishment *they're* handing out." There he went, blaming people for shit before he even knew the facts. Not unlike most cops, but more than a girlfriend could handle, hence being broken up.

"Hm, yeah, blood in, blood out," I mindlessly replied. The hardening of my heart was a process that had been hard at work for years.

"Funny. So, ideas?"

"Well, I'd start with Reggie's nearest and dearest, but oh wait, I killed them. I don't know Mike, I'm on fucking vacation." Technically, I was on a research expedition, but it was vacation-like and I was using it to its fullest. As best as I could without the aid of my dipshit travel companion. He'd picked the absolute wrong time to solicit help from me.

"Yes, I know. You're on vacation with the exact people I think are involved in this. Each of the girls was connected somehow to a Sanguinarian club or group, or whatever the fuck you call them."

"House. It's usually called a House. Don't you watch TV?" I was suddenly exhausted. Talking to Mike about dead girls made my head want to go to sleep for an awfully long time.

"Humph." He made a sucking sound with his teeth, and I knew he was judging me. He was bad about that. "Do you have an idea how to go about getting information?"

I shrugged. "I guess I can… wait! No, no, no. No more dead girls. No more gore. No more death. Please," I dropped my head into my free hand and held it tight.

"No more gore and death? Aren't you about two hours away from entering Satan's asshole? You don't want this, well guess what, baby, you got it. Right in your fucking lap. You hunted the devil down the first time around. This time you're blindly jumping into the bullshit with both feet. And to make matters worse, you're a four-hour flight away. There's nothing I can do if something happens." His voice gave away his facial expression. I could picture him with his furrowed brow and tightly set jaw.

"That's what this is all about? You're all pissy pants because I hauled off and left the state. I'm not there at your beck and call, vampire kids in tow. I brought down the baddies last time, sweetheart, this time you're on your own. You and all those other idiot fucking cops need to do your goddamn jobs before another girl turns up without her head." More than anger, my voice held a viciousness intended to strike low and do damage.

"Dylan, you can be such a fucking bitch." Expression change. Brows lifted in the center and eyes set on puppy dog. I knew that asshole way too damn well.

"That's right, baby, get over it." I hung up. For the sixth time since I'd known him, I hung up on him.

My hands were a bit shaky with adrenaline and I needed a stiff one. A drink. A stiff drink.

More dead girls. Fucking wonderful. I felt for the poor little headless girls, really I did, but in the end, I still had *my* head.

Well, for now.

FIVE

WE PARKED IN A FAIRLY ORDINARY PARKING LOT CENTERED between a few interesting buildings. The smell of dank canal water hit me as soon as I stepped foot out of the rental car. It smelled like old tap water and fish. I wrinkled up my nose in disgust before I realized that was probably offensive. I ran my hand across my nose and glanced around at my company to make sure no one saw me. Malcolm had seen every second of the little dance and scowled at my inconsiderate gesture. My defensive nature kicked in and I threw him a stink eye. I didn't like Malcolm McTavish much to begin with, and I was always looking for a reason to dislike him even more. Letting him know that, was just added pleasure.

A large crowd was gathering on the sidewalk on the perimeter of the parking lot. At first, I thought maybe someone had fainted or went into labor. Once we got a little closer, I was able to see a small sign propped on the ground. Ghost Tours, it read in white chalk. Not quite as dramatic as the scene I'd had in mind.

I'd never proclaimed myself as an avid horror buff, but I'd always been intrigued by the paranormal. Probably one of the deep-seated reasons I chose to research the Vampire Massacres and allowed myself to get tangled up with the underground vamp scene in the first place. Down deep in my core, I liked the unknown, and the thought of searching for haunts in New Orleans sounded downright amazing. I knew damn good and well not one of the folks in my party was about to ditch out on our evening with the plastic-fanged ones to hear tales of local bumps in the night . My inner child pouted a bit at the thought of not getting what I wanted.

If I survive the night, I'm ghost hunting tomorrow if it kills me.

"Where is it we're going?" I whined, just a little.

"We'll have quite a walk I'm afraid. I thought Tatum and yourself would like to see a few sights on our way to our first stop." Malcolm, such a pompous ass, gave a look that was meant just for me. It said, what's wrong, fatty, can't keep up?

Fucker.

"Sugar tits, I'm not really wearing walking shoes here. It would've been nice to know we'd be headed out on a trek across the French Quarter." I strutted ahead of him with fat chick determination. All ass and wiggle.

"Ugh, I wish you two would just beat the shit out of each other and see who wins. But I like you both too damn much to watch either of you bleed," Tatum's voice called from just behind me.

Malcolm scoffed, and I pictured him walking behind me with that stupid look he got on his face like he's so much better than everyone else. I immediately thought of Philippe, Diego, whatever, and the bloody mess I'd made of him. Poor little vampire boy. I smiled a terribly sinister smile when my mind placed Malcolm's head on Philippe's gory body. Sometimes, not always, but sometimes, I frightened myself.

"Here," Tatum flung a pair of thin roll-up flats over my shoulder and forced me to snap out of psycho-land.

"Thanks," I said as I jerked the stupid shoes from her hand. It wasn't nice, I was aware, but who really fucking cared in the end. She'd been careening toward the top of my shit list for a while.

"Give me your hand." Cyrus stood next to me, and I allowed him to hold my arm while I took off my three-inch heels and replaced them with the lifesaving flats.

Normally, I would have protested, even in the most moderate sense, at permitting Cyrus to aid me in any way, but I was too stubborn to allow myself to look like more of a fool by falling on my face trying to change shoes all by my lonesome. Honestly, I was much happier without the stupid heels on, but I was left to carry the damn things.

"Please." Cyrus reached a long-fingered hand out and gently took the shoes from my white-knuckled clutch.

I was so taken back by his unsolicited chivalry, I let go of the shoes and stared at him. A beautiful white smile spread across his face in a grin that was just as attractive as it was threatening. I'd always suspected Cyrus Atossa as the predator type, but I could never put my finger on why. The more time I spent with him, the more I realized someone that perfect had to be either stupid or deadly; there was rarely a gray area in those types of situations. And I'd be damned, the boy wasn't stupid.

I shook off my feeling of astonishment and walked on, reveling in my newfound comfort. Although I still wished I was wearing my sneakers.

Walking the streets of the infamous French Quarter it was nothing like I expected it to be. I'd always made the idiotic assumption it was a tourist trap filled with college students and drunk topless girls. Apparently, that was exclusive to Mardi Gras and Tijuana. I was slightly disappointed. Not that I'd ever let the *girls* fly free in public, merely a prime opportunity to throw stuff at ridiculous people.

Instead of tourists and too much booze, I found locals and sightseers all mingled together in the hustle and bustle of the closing of the business day. The sun was setting and many shops were preparing to close for the night or were turning on lamps and lights to announce their presence to passersby. A few shops were decorated for Halloween with paper ghosts and macabre décor. It was also likely that was their everyday décor. I couldn't be certain.

I passed a small shop with long strings of beads dangling in the doorway. The actual door had been propped open with a clearly heavy brass statue of someone I didn't recognize. The spicy scent that wafted from the opening called to me. A terrace jutted out over the entry from the floor above and held a wooden sign that read, Madam Azelie. Scattered symbols carved into the sign intrigued me more than they should have. I assumed that was the intent.

A standing sign out front told me this was the place to get inexpensive psychic "readin's " and *charms*. Without asking a soul in my group, I made the quick turn from the sidewalk and pushed through the beaded doorway. Always the rebel.

The wooden beads slapped together with a dull clank as I passed through them. The room was a perfect square, painted terracotta, and filled to the brim with as many candles and satchels and dolls as one tiny little room could hold. Odd mixes of Catholic symbols, such as crucifixes, hung from the ceiling and statues of an odd-looking Virgin Mary were surrounded by clay forms of naked humans and candles in the shape of the grim reaper. Wooden masks hung at various intervals on the packed walls and tufts of feathers poked from the tops of jars. It appeared to be a shop, but nothing was marked with a price.

Puffs of smoke pulsed in odd cadence from an unseen source behind a counter covered in painted fabric. The distinct sound of a record player scratched out unknown drumbeats from somewhere in the back. The muddling of sensory overload made my head swoon a bit with a feeling of disorientation.

A teeny tiny girl emerged from behind a colorful silk curtain in a far back corner. Her smile welcomed me, but the aura she projected was all power that tingled over my skin. I respected that and smiled back, allowing my suddenly fast heartbeat to slow to a more manageable pace.

"Aye, dawlin'. What bring you here?" Her voice was a rolling hiss in her quasi-French accent you rarely heard anywhere but in Louisiana.

"Actually, your nifty sign out front," I said, shifting uncomfortably on my feet.

The small woman stared at me through a thick caking of charcoal eye makeup. Her dark dreadlocks were pulled loosely to the crown of her head into a thick poof, held together with a skinny strip of leather. The stark contrast of her nearly black hair against her creamed butter skin was breathtaking, but the sky-blue eyes peering out at me from black smudges on her lids scared the shit out of me.

"Your future you seek?" She slithered toward me like a snake on two legs. Those blue eyes looked me up and down as her head shifted on slender shoulders. Curling upward from the neckline of her bohemian crop top, a black-inked tattoo nestled neatly in her modest cleavage that reached up her neck. Simple, single lines creating some kind of symbol I wasn't familiar with, but in the same vein as those on her sign out front.

Two shiny silver rings adorned her nose and her ears were filled from the lobe up with oddly shaped rings and plugs. She had beautiful skin. Other than the eyes, she didn't seem to be wearing any makeup. Or it may have been the dim light brought from the kerosene lamps that hung from sconces on each wall. I wondered why Mr. Edison had skipped out on this particular establishment but decided it was best not to ask. Like me, she may have been a Tesla girl.

Her intense eyes felt like they were crawling on my skin, traipsing over every inch of me with her stare. "A charm? For protection m'be?"

Her voice didn't quite match her body. A near baritone, speech slipped out with an accent I pegged as Cajun, or as close to it as I could recognize anyhow. I wasn't really good at that sort of thing. Just ask Dominika the Hungarian and her Russian accent.

"Do I need protecting?" I asked, honestly concerned she knew something I didn't. I'd heard of people like that. People that could sense death coming. I didn't necessarily believe in that sort of thing, but if someone were to tell me I was going to die in a bus accident on a Friday, I'd likely not ride a bus on Fridays for a while. Just in case.

The little woman stepped back away from me a few steps.

"Protection you have." Her head snaked again, and her eyes focused over my shoulder.

A second later, I heard the distinct sound of wooden beads softly clanking against each other. I turned to find Tatum in the doorway. Cyrus stood behind her, nearly beside, but Malcolm peered over their shoulders from the street. *Pussy.*

"Hey, Dylan, let's go," Tatum said from the doorway.

"Yes, let's," Cyrus agreed from over her shoulder looking overly concerned.

I rolled my eyes and ignored them both. "My future. I'd like you to read my future." I turned to the girl and nodded my head confidently.

"Come, *'cher*," the girl beckoned me with a crook of her finger.

I followed her behind a silk curtain and away from my friends. No one said a word. Not one of them tried to stop me. So, fuck 'em.

"A man… two men?" she asked over her shoulder before she even sat down.

"No men," I said with a smirk.

"Yeah, heaps and heaps." She smiled right back as the two of us sat across a small round table from each other, my back facing the entranceway that led to the public area of the store.

In the center of the table, sat a rectangular shaped object wrapped in fancy silk fabric. The girl's child-like hand reached across the table and took the silky block from the center. One hand was wrapped with a simple black rosary that dangled between her fingers. The cross that hung from it dragged along the table as she moved about. She unwrapped the hidden shape and revealed it to be a deck of cards. My moderate knowledge of the occult told me it was likely a set of tarot cards.

"Take 'dis and hold it tight," she handed me the stack of cards and pushed my hands toward my chest. "Make a thought of what you want or a question you need answerin'. Focus. Then cut the deck two times." The miniature girl sat across from me with the stillness of a marble statue. Her bare arms showed more tattoos trailing from her wrists up to her naked shoulders. Each one similar to the one on her chest, several kinds of symbols, like those I'd seen on her sign. More charms and shapes dangled from gold wires and brown leather strips wrapped in her neatly matted dreads.

I followed her instructions and thought hard about my question. My mind raced with the question I refused to even ask myself. Over and over images of Cyrus's beautiful green eyes and Mike's adorable ass dimples came through my thoughts. I forced myself to concentrate on the overall subject I wanted answers for. *Where is my life going?* I took a deep breath in and slowly let it out through pursed lips.

"Cut twice and hand it back," she said, breaking the momentary silence as if she knew just when my mind had been made up.

Without further words, the girl took the deck and began dealing them across the table in an intricate pattern, her crucifix dragging along the silk table covering. One on top of the other, then to the side, to the north and the south, then at random in a straight line. The cards depicted images in crude, thick line drawings and paint; a woman sitting atop a throne, a man holding a bunch of sticks, a child on a horse, a man stepping off the edge of a cliff. I watched diligently, hoping to decipher what was coming across the cards. I had nothing. Unless I was going to become a queen and order men to build me things and leap from cliff edges. No, nothing.

"How the hell is this supposed to tell me my future?" I asked, mostly to myself. In fact, I really hadn't expected to say it out loud.

"Not your future, *'cher*, your path. A path can be changed. The future is loosely defined," she spoke without looking up from the cards.

"You don't believe in fate? Destiny and all that?" I asked a bit too smugly.

The girl let out a scoff, "Ah, fate. You said future. Fate comes as it wills. Nothin' moves fate." Her eyes moved over each card, reading them, as far as I could tell. "From the city of angels, I see," she said and moved on without waiting for my response. "You seen death." Again, a statement not a question. "On your hands, blood," a slender finger lifted from the card and waved in the air in front of my face. "Tsk, Tsk, Tsk, naughty girl."

"What? What do you see?" I wiggled in my seat at the thought of her possibly knowing the ins and outs of the deaths of two young men at my hand. Mike had pulled a ton of strings and got me off the hook, but that's not to say it wouldn't come right back and bite me in the ass someday. This day.

"I see death… and you. And blood. Yours… and others. Lust. Greed. Sex," her eyes never left the cards. It was like she was seeing things in her head I couldn't. Regardless of her apparent concentration on the cards, it was obvious her focus was wide spread throughout the room.

It was my turn to scoff. "Sex? Yeah, right," I said, trying to ignore the tightness I was beginning to feel being stuck in that tiny back room.

"Don't mock, just listen," her small hand lifted as she spoke and waved, beckoning me to focus on her. It worked. My eyes shifted attention to her face. "You're with those not of your kind. Discomfort. Betrayal. Your path shifted," her head turned to the side eerily similar to that of a bird hunting its prey. Listening to something I couldn't hear. "'Cause death done come through your house. The dead surround you now." Her eyes lifted from the layout of cards to glare into mine, "Murder… and magic bring you here."

"Ha ha, what?" I laughed nervously. "What are you talking about?"

"You…" Her eyes penetrated my guard and pulled at my thoughts. I could feel her prodding inside my head. "You bring death in my house. Blood on your hands. Blood of the dead come wit'chu where you go. Why you seek me?" Her train of thought switched so suddenly I almost didn't catch it.

"I saw your sign. I was walking with my friends and I saw your sign. I don't know"—I shrugged—"I just came in." The tiny girl held a stare that would make a lesser man shit his pants. Luckily for me, I was a woman.

Her eyes narrowed, and I felt her delve deeper into my head. I'd never been to a supposed psychic before, but I was pretty certain that was not the norm. "Meurtrière," she said in a near whisper.

"What? No, what are you talking about?" I pleaded, plotting my expedient exit should shit hit the proverbial fan.

The girl inhaled dramatically and stood in one fell swoop. "Murderess!" Her miniature finger came up to point at me with such vengeance I felt the force in my soul.

"You're fucking nuts!" I stood too. For the first time in my twenty-odd years, I felt two particular things at once , horrendous fear and pretty damn tall.

When I stood, my chair toppled over and hit the cement

floor with a wooden clatter. In a heartbeat, I heard the beads at the front door and felt a rush of electricity as another being entered the room. Cyrus wrapped his thick arm around my waist and pulled me backward out of the tiny backroom. All the while, the girl with the dreadlocks cursed me violently in an unintelligible mix of English and some form of French. It wasn't the first time someone chewed me out in a foreign language and it likely wouldn't be the last.

"Put me down, goddammit!" I wailed and kicked my feet at his shins.

Admittedly, I didn't kick as hard as I could have. I didn't want to bruise the poor boy. But I sure as hell wanted him to let me free so I could take my vengeance on the little woman still cursing my future grandchildren in her odd language. I should have been afraid, hell, terrified, but all I wanted to do was rip her tiny little head off. In my defense, I tended to transform fear into sheer rage. It was sort of a habit. We were halfway down the block in a matter of seconds, Cyrus still holding me with little effort around my waist. I fought and screamed all the way.

"Are you stupid?" Cyrus let me go with such force I stumbled backward and nearly fell on my ass.

"Fuck you, asshole." My hair was a hot mess from being pressed so closely to him, and my dress was bunched around my hips exposing my thick thighs and the bottom of my butt cheeks. He looked me up and down and I quickly adjusted the dress and made an attempt at the hair.

"Do you know what she is?" His intensity only worsened my fear. I mean rage. "This isn't a game, Dylan!"

"What the fuck are you talking about?" My feet nearly left the pavement as the rest of my body reacted to the inertia of me yelling.

"That girl in that shop believes with everything in her soul she has power. You can taste it on the air the second you enter the beaded doorway. She's a priestess, Dylan. A high priestess… if I had to guess. And she has it out for you now."

"And how do you know that? Because she saw it in her little cards?"

"No, because she cursed your *house* while I was dragging you out of the room," Cyrus said as he towered over me like he was my father.

"Oh and all of a sudden you speak French?" And apparently Hungarian.

"No, I speak English, and so does she. Enough of it for me to understand you've made an enemy in your first hour in the city. Way to go." He paced around me.

"Shit, sorry. I was unaware I was supposed to sit idly by while some little girl accuses me of murder."

"She didn't accuse you, to be accused she'd have to be wrong, or at least presumably wrong. You *are* a murderer, of sorts. You killed two boys and she knows it." Tatum, who'd been meandering, with her stupid ginger boyfriend, down the street to meet us, piped in with her two cents.

"Who asked you?" I turned to glare at my absentee friend. "Maybe if you'd bothered to glance up from that freckled bloodsucker, you could've stopped me, but apparently it doesn't matter what time zone we're in, you're still shoved so far up his ass you can taste his haggis." I stamped my foot against the cracked pavement and moved my vengeance toward the Persian. "And how did she know what'd happened? You're telling me she's a psychic? A priestess *and* psychic? Well, fuck me with a flip flop, eh?" I flapped my arms at my sides unattractively and let out an even less attractive huff.

"You're the idiot that went into a voodoo shop in New Orleans," Tatum shrugged her shoulders as if she were talking about washing a red sock with the whites. She didn't even acknowledge my blatant attack on her and her new found relationship. No big deal. "Why the hell did you go in there in the first place? I never knew mysticism was your thing." She turned her head coyly as her ridiculous boyfriend kissed her neck.

"Are you on drugs?" I asked without expecting an answer; Cyrus laughed. "I don't know why I went in. I'm in fucking New Orleans. What else is there? Ghost tours, voodoo, and apparently red headed vampire boys who can't stop sucking face with my friend." No response. "Jesus, I saw the sign. I liked the symbols. Besides, I'd do pretty much anything to get away from this bullshit." I lifted my hand and used all my fingers at once to point in the direction of the disgusting show of public affection.

No response. I'd followed Tatum halfway across the country taking her at her word that all she wanted was to spend time with me. To ensure I had fun. To pull me out of the gun-toting funk I'd slipped into since becoming a murderess and full-time author. I'd been with them just over seven hours, including the flight, and all I'd seen of her is the side of her face as it was suctioned tightly to the face of Vlad the Ginger Kid. I had half a mind to pack my shit and head right back to my dungeon. Gun and all.

"Darling, please make better choices in the future. I'd hate to see you lose that pretty head of yours." Cyrus took his strong hands and held my face gently between them. I felt instant calm wash over me. Warm hands and pretty green eyes had that effect on people.

Maybe I can stay for the weekend.

I let out a short laugh, "Ironically, that comment just may come to fruition if I keep hanging with the likes of you." Cyrus gave me an inquisitive look, hands still cradling my face. "I got a call from Mike." The look changed to disdain. "Told me to be safe. Another headless corpse popped up in Texas. Making eight including Reggie. Staked, hands bound with hair, all girls, all affiliated with the vampire subculture." I don't know what came over me to explain all this to the likes of Cyrus Atossa, but it all just spilled out.

"Ah, I remember this girl. This is the journalist I met at Macabre Saturnine so many months ago. This is the girl who's all business. Always just out for the story. I'd think eight headless girls would make a better tale than a little vampire party." He was right. I just didn't have it in me to see more death. At least not for a while.

I backed out of his hands and stood a few feet away. "No, no more true crime. I'm here for the fiction and the free trip. Although, after *that* encounter, I may start researching magic and mystics." A familiar smile spread across my face. It was the smile of horrible ideas fermenting in my ever-working mind.

"Embracing the occult I see. I don't think magic will do you well. You seem to make enemies easily and those types of people are not the kind you want as enemies."

"The occult?" The cogs started moving of their own will in my head. "That has promise." My thoughts were not always positive. Shit, half the time they could be downright horrendous.

I let my mind spin out of control with thoughts of the occult as I followed Cyrus when he turned down the street and walked away from me. Eventually, Tatum and Malcolm made their way to lead the pack to our destination. Walking arm and arm, Tatum and Malcolm were oblivious to the world around them. As was I, to a point. I had visions of headless, psychic sugarplums dancing in my head. Fiction books based on all things occult. So many aspects to cover. So many opportunities. So many terrible situations to get myself into along the way, all in the name of research.

Maybe I could write a memoir of my research. Who the hell would read a book series like that?

SIX

A FIFTEEN-MINUTE-WALK THROUGH THE STREETS OF NEW Orleans took us to our destination. A two-story Victorian teahouse smack-dab in the middle of the hustle and bustle of the French Quarter.

The sun had nearly set leaving the sky a gradient of blue that ranged from royal to nearly white nearest the setting sun behind the horizon. Night had come to New Orleans and we, the four of us, were just getting started.

"Hiding in plain sight, are we?" I said with a snarky tone. I hadn't even experienced anything yet, and I already wanted to go home.

"I am allowing you to attend a *very* exclusive summit. You will meet those of my kind and you will behave appropriately." Malcolm spoke to me as if I was so beneath him he wouldn't spit on me to save my life.

"Or what? You'll give me a spanking?" I raised one defiant brow.

"*I* might," Cyrus smiled widely, and I blushed and moved on.

A set of small front steps led us to a covered patio lined with hanging strings of charms and pendants, each a different color and symbol. I tried to eye all of them individually. That was the type of minute detail I needed for a killer fiction novel. Who'd have guessed you could find something like that in the backwoods streets of downtown New Orleans?

"Each House is represented," Cyrus said from nowhere as if reading my mind. "This is Malcolm's House, Cailleadh," he pointed to a braided Celtic cross that held a green stone in the center. It was only one of well over a dozen hanging charms that were collected on the eaves of the porch. Others were shaped like Ankhs, or crosses, or stars. I wondered what the other Houses were called. "Each House has a Primus and each Primus has a Secondus. You'll be meeting them all." His eyes shifted to the door. "Right about... now."

The ornate door opened. The streetlamp shone eerily across the face of our greeter. She was so tall she made Tatum look like... well... me. Red locks were pulled back tightly in a bun that made all her features more prominent than was attractive. The light cast shadows across her face that caused it to look monstrous instead of human. She wore a shiny black latex bodysuit complete with thigh-high stilettos. She looked as though she was getting ready to slip through a tight space and not attend a business meeting. But then again, I was not the expert in the vampire soirée attire category.

Malcolm stepped to the door and extended his hand to the woman towering over him. She said something I didn't understand and leaned a great distance to kiss Malcolm across his knuckles. It struck me as odd that a woman would be kissing a man's hand, but again, not the expert.

No more formalities followed with the oversized woman. Malcolm and Tatum walked in a strange fashion through the door, entering at the same time. Cyrus extended his arm as escort and I reluctantly took it. The woman waited at the doorway with her eyes to the ground. I smiled in her direction, but she never acknowledged anyone but Malcolm. She closed the door behind us swiftly, moving around our group to the heavy black drapes that led elsewhere. Her slender fingers tugged a rope to raise the drapes, revealing a second space.

"Master, Malcolm McTavish, Primus, House of Cailleadh, Los Angeles. Escort, Tatum Price." Malcolm and Tatum waited at the entrance to the other room as the latex girl announced their presence. The two moved into the space where a large group of others were gathered. "Sir, Cyrus Atossa, Secondus, House of Cailleadh, Los Angeles. Escort, Dylan Hart." The girl introduced us as if she'd been reading from a list of guests. Maybe she had memorized the damn thing.

Eyes wide in shock, I lowered my brows and looked at Cyrus. He'd mentioned Secondus, talked like it was some kind of right-hand man, a second in command; he never said it was *him*. I always thought he was some kind of lackey. A minion to do bidding and carry luggage. If he was a second in command, they must have a strange way of honoring that. Cyrus pulled his shoulders back and led the way through the black curtains. All the while, I stared at him with wide eyes and a gaping mouth.

Once inside, we were greeted by a line of strangely dressed vampire folk. Not one of them seemed to be representing the same period or genre. Malcolm and Tatum obviously represented LA chic; the charcoal black suit with an emerald green tie and a floor length green crushed velvet dress worked well for the two. The others weren't quite so blessed with such glorious fashion sense. One couple donned Victorian garb that matched the teahouse, another matched the latex girl at the front door, and yet another couple of women wore all white lace down to their delicate fans. I looked down at my understated little black dress and instantly felt underdressed. Especially in my flats. I snuck a glance to Cyrus' other hand and smiled from ear to ear when I saw my sexy black heels dangling from his fingers.

Tapping on his shoulder, I pointed to his hidden hand and my much-needed shoes. He smiled and sneakily handed me one at a time. No one was paying any attention to the two of us anyway; they were all focused on Malcolm and his new fancy American girlfriend. Shoes firmly attached to my feet, I stuck the roll-up flats in my purse and proceeded with the evening.

Malcolm followed along the line the other guests had established when we were announced to the room. He and Tatum shook hands and kissed knuckles with every last individual. Following Cyrus's lead, I did the same. I heard so many names as I kissed and shook. I had no clue what the fuck I was doing, but I was doing it. I felt so unbelievably out of place in my little black Macy's dress and clearance heels. I just wanted to go home and put on my pajamas. But all the vampire hierarchy information I was soaking in just being in the presence of those people was worth the discomfort. With every introduction, I built new characters. With each glance at the layout of the teahouse, I created vivid scenes in my head. A fiction book was what I had in mind and what better to inspire fiction than reality?

We'd reached the end of the line, and I stood there hanging in space with nothing to do and no one directing me to the next activity. Cyrus held his arm out for me once again and once again I took it. I felt better being connected to him. I felt less vulnerable. If there was anything in the world I hated being, it was vulnerable. All right, there were a shitload of things I hated, but vulnerability was probably in the top three. It was a subset of fear.

The group, at least ten Houses from what I could gather, each with a Primus and a Secondus, and some with escorts, made the cozy room feel downright snug. There weren't many seating areas in the Victorian decorated room, so I stood. And I waited. For what? I had no clue. Something. There had to be a reason for all the formality.

A second door opened at the far wall and light spilled into the dimly lit room. Another latex wearing girl stood at the doorway without a sound. Her eyes focused on the floor at her feet. She stood motionless as the others moved past her into the adjacent room. The latex girls appeared to be the help. The help shoved into skintight shiny suits. I sincerely hoped no one expected me to squeeze my dimply ass into one of those suits to tote around luggage.

I welcomed the new space. The dining room was five times

the size of the other. Almost in the dead center sat an elegant formal dining table with enough chairs surrounding it to seat everyone in attendance. Tall white candles twinkled throughout the room and cluttered the table in intentional chaos. Ivory plates sat atop brushed gold chargers. Brass rings held burgundy cloth napkins. Each place setting was marked with a card with a name scrawled across it.

Assigned seating, great.

I waited and watched the crowd as they moved, as if in a dance, to their respective seats. For the most part, each member of each House sat together. I felt Cyrus adjust his weight to walk and I followed his lead. He found our names with little effort, conveniently right next to each other. If I was being honest, I wasn't exactly heartbroken I had to sit next to the man for the evening. He smelled nice and seemed to be team Dylan. I was curious as to why he and I had been placed together from nearly the moment we'd gotten on the plane. My gut told me it was completely intentional.

Malcolm sat to the left of our group with Tatum between Malcolm and me, thank God. There was obviously a pattern hidden in the seating arrangement. I made a mental note to ask Cyrus as many questions as I could about the formalities of the culture when we were alone. Then I thought momentarily about being alone with Cyrus. Then I blushed and thought about something else. Anything else.

The center of the long table was covered in an ivory silk cloth as long as I was tall. Assuming the cloth covered our would-be dinner, I didn't think too much of it and waited for the next social cue. All the guests lifted their napkins and placed them in their laps. Not abnormal behavior, I followed suit. When everyone sat quietly, I did too. I did everything short of breathe in the same cadence just to make sure I didn't stand out as an outsider.

It was odd that I was involved in any of the community meetings in the first place. Other than the fact that my best friend was screwing the Primus of the House of whatever, I saw no reason for my ass to be placed uncomfortably in their really old and likely expensive dining chair. But I didn't complain. Nope. I sat there and shut the fuck up, for once. I'd seen enough of the supposed vampire world that it didn't shock me anymore. It was intriguing. And they all frightened me just enough to watch my ass.

The two latex girls came into the room carrying silver platters with many pewter goblets balanced on them. They handed out the drinks one by one and left the room promptly when finished. Without thinking, I lifted my glass to inspect the contents. I eagerly hoped it was full of some kind of delicious alcohol. Cyrus made a low noise in his throat and moved his head. It was so slight I barely caught his expression. He was telling me to put my glass down and behave. I did.

No one else had lifted their cup. Each member of the group sat motionless in wait of something I was unaware. One of the white lace ladies, I recognized her as the one who I'd thought was Dominika, stood at her seat and lifted her cup. No one else followed, so I didn't either. At that distance, she really didn't look that much like Dominika. She didn't have the word cunt stamped in bright red ink across her face. Just another striking face in the sea of pretty people.

"Welcome to all in attendance. My gratitude to every lord and lady and the house of which they represent. As Primus of the House of Porte, representing New Orleans, and the Southern Cabal, I embrace you all into our community. Please, eat as you will, drink freely, and enjoy your stay." She made eye contact with each of us before moving on, "A toast…" Everyone raised their glasses. "To reverence and mien. To collaboration and distinction. To love… and lust." The woman in lace tilted her cup toward Cyrus and me. "May the future meet you with life and power until the day your life should cease. Blessed be!" The woman in white lace delicately tilted her cup and drank. Everyone followed a second later, as did I.

The woman sat, but as she did, she lifted her lace-gloved hand and snapped dainty fingers. A moment later, latex girls hurried through the darkened doorway they had disappeared through previously. Each took a place at opposite ends of the table. With practiced flourish, the two removed the silk cloth to reveal our buffet.

The body of a naked woman lay motionless in the center of the table. Light shimmered on her dark skin like sweating chocolate. Her long hair had been intentionally placed around her head to look as though it was flowing around her. My mind flashed on a headless Reggie, naked hookers in black and white, glugging gallons of blood drenching a damp basement. Adrenaline took over and I couldn't breathe. Without my control, my body pushed itself back into the chair as far as it would go and my eyes closed tight. I waited to hear Tatum react. Nothing. Seconds passed that felt like minutes. A round of applause rolled lightly through the room, but no reaction of terror. No screams.

No gasps of horror.

Shit. Naked bitches on the table cannot be a good thing.

I forced my eyes open, searching the room. Victorian clad heads of staff dined on intricately wrapped pieces of sushi. Each fanged mouth gobbled up rice and seaweed like it was their last meal. In shock, I looked at the dark-skinned woman on the table. Covering her flat stomach, ample chest, and protruding hip bones were little pieces of sushi and other edibles. Her eyes were closed and her lips parted naturally, but she was breathing normal controlled breaths. A living, breathing, food canvas. In that moment, I was both relieved and disappointed. I was quite ready to Quinton Tarantino my way out of a den of bloodsuckers. Plus, what kind of vampire colony sat around and ate raw fish and rice?

I didn't eat anything that once touched someone's naked flesh as a rule, so I quietly sipped from my fancy pewter glass. No one had seemed to notice my quiet spectacle, and I was glad for that. I wasn't really ready to explain to a room full of plastic fanged blood drinkers that I thought perhaps they were serving up a pretty little Creole girl for dinner.

I watched as the pleasantries continued. The little vampires played nice, drank their respective liquids from their fancy glasses, ate stinky fish from the flesh of the naked girl on the table, and I prayed they'd be serving something edible soon.

Cyrus spoke only when spoken to, and I noticed most of the other Secondus' did as well. Malcolm was holding a superficial conversation with a woman to his left and Tatum sat there looking pretty, as she did so well. The Victorian-clad man sitting across and to my right stared down my dress as often as he could, and a woman across the table from me watched him with a crooked brow. Other than the weird clothes and the naked girl, it seemed like any other business dinner I'd ever attended. The hostess welcomed her guests, made a toast to teamwork, and fed everyone food and drink. The only suspiciously odd thing was the obvious line drawn in the sand between Primus and Secondus. Oh, and the plastic fangs. It seemed ridiculous to me why anyone would take this game of dress up so damn seriously. Serious to the point of allowing yourself to be treated as a second-class citizen all in the name of bloody hierarchy. It was probably why I was single and worked for myself. Lack of appreciation for authority and chain of command. Damn the man. Save the Empire.

A warm hand slid over mine that rested on the soft linen tablecloth. I turned to see Cyrus's tanned hand run reassuringly across the back of mine. It wasn't a lingering touch, just something to let me know I wasn't alone in the room. I smiled in his direction but received nothing in return. His eyes stayed fixed on the others around the table. It seemed to me like he was watching each conversation, eavesdropping in a sly little way. I guessed one could discover a load of new things he could use against people if one just shut the fuck up and listened.

Clever.

An hour passed and I had been served a delicious soup full of rice and a spicy sausage, a thick slab of medium rare steak, and a hefty serving of red beans and rice. I felt like I was going to explode. I had no clue the evening was going to begin so hospitably.

The social veil had lifted by the second course and almost

everybody was talking and getting to know the newbies. Mostly the escorts. It was obvious the nitty-gritty political background was either nonexistent or not discussed with strangers present. I got the feeling the entire weekend was a superficial gathering to allow the community to socialize, and create a huge money-making opportunity for all by including the public in most of the events. The summit in the teahouse was not one of those public events obviously. I felt a bit honored to be in a position of trust that I was invited to join in. How I'd attained such an honor was still up in the air. As time went on, I began to doubt Tatum had that kind of pull. I had so many questions running through my head. I wanted to ask them all, but it was clear most of them would go unanswered or end me as coffin bait.

I had thought for a moment before we left LA about bringing my new voice recorder. After I lost the first, and with it a shit ton of research, I'd become more cautious about where I toted that thing around. It was also possible I may have been discovered as a mole and eaten alive. Not a good way to go out. I forced my brain to take mental notes of every face, of every tidbit of information I'd heard, no matter how minuscule it may have been. As soon as I was free of prying eyes, I'd scribble everything into my own handy dandy notebook. Thankfully, there wasn't much alcohol present, thus no way for me to become too inebriated to recall the events. Which had been an issue in the past.

Our hostess, whom I learned was Marienne, the Primus of Louisiana, thanked us all once again at the end of our meal. With a dramatic lift of her goblet, she gave her final toast for the evening.

"My fellowship, another summit has passed and with it another year of peaceful existence. We gathered today as many branches of one tree. Tall, we stand, branches outstretched, immovable and unshakable." She looked at Malcolm. "Unbreakable. Let not the events of this year taint the next. Blessed be all who dine with me." She held her glass up for a long-distance toast with everyone at the table one by one and gulped down her last drop. We all followed suit, and it appeared the summit was over.

"That's it? What now?" I asked quietly as everyone began to stand after our hostess stood and left the room.

"Now, we dance," Cyrus said with a wiggle of his brow.

"And drink?" I replied with a huge grin.

Keep it to one, Dylan Hart.

"Oh, yes." He wrapped an arm around my waist pulled me into his warm body.

A tingly sensation ran from my chest to my butt cheeks the second my body touched his. It wasn't like me to be filled with uncontrollable sexual tension, but desperate times called for desperate measures. It'd been the longest dry spell of my life but in no way did a tryst with the gorgeous Cyrus Atossa count as a moment of desperation. Not on my end anyway. If I could've, I would've given myself a fist bump.

Holy sexcapades, Batman!

The other guests filed from the room, but Cyrus and I stood at our places, his arm enveloping my thick midsection with not an ounce of hesitation.

"Let's book it, kiddies. We've got a party to get to." Tatum had poked her head back into the room and shouted from the doorway to the only two people left.

I let out a breath, slow and even. Cyrus and I moved to the door in succession with Malcolm and Tatum. Everyone moved through the front parlor and out the front door into the city night. Music filled the air and the smell of cooking food wafted from every corner. The guests that had once crowded the little parlor poured into the street. All walking with their assigned groups they'd arrived with. All donning their choice of vampire apparel.

Standing on the porch of the tea house, I watched as a horde of vampires descended on New Orleans. Without hesitation, I followed that horde. I followed and smiled.

I'm a fucking idiot.

SEVEN

I WALKED ARM AND ARM WITH THE LOVELY CYRUS ATOSSA through the cooling night. The crowd of vampires had spread to either side of the street. Sidewalks and streets scattered with plastic fanged blood drinkers. No one batted an eye. The group had been wandering the streets about five minutes when my phone vibrated in my bra. The noise sounded like a fart and Cyrus looked down at me concerned. I chuckled nervously and reached down into my boobs to retrieve the buzzing phone.

"Yeah?" I said with as much annoyance as I could.

"Dylan, honey?"

"Mom." *Crap*. "Hi. Sorry I didn't call when I got in. I got—"

She cut me off. “It’s okay, I know you’re trying to have fun. Honey, I saw on the news about another case like your friend. The girl with the… you know… head lopped off. The lady on the news said the girls are linked to underground vampire clubs.” Her raspy voice, though truck stop waitress-esque, held a tone of concern that could make even the toughest criminal pack their bags and head out on that guilt trip.

“Mom, yeah, don’t worry about that.” I reassured her of my safety even though I wasn’t totally certain of it myself.

“Well, I called Mike. Just to be sure.”

“Fuck, Mom, really?” Those were a few of the worst words she could have said to me.

“Fuck, *Dylan*, yes. He’s worried about you. And so am I. You know, you’d be much better off letting Tatum live that lifestyle alone. I know you love her, but she’s an adult, and so are you. You don’t have to follow that girl anymore. Especially if she’s dragging you along to places where girls are getting beheaded. Christ, just six months ago those vampire kids were killing those girls right here in town and look where that got you.”

Bags packed, ticket purchased, we’re going on a guilt trip.

“Ugh, mom, I’m fine. Please stop talking to Michael. He’s an idiot.” Okay, not an idiot, just overbearing.

“He loves you.” Only a mother knows exactly how to open up those old wounds.

I might need my passport for this trip.

“Jesus. Yes, I know, but it doesn’t matter. His issue is not with the case, it’s with me. His brain catches on fire anytime I’m five feet away from him. Always has been, always will be a controlling asshole."

"Worry and control are very different. If you'd think for just one second before you hauled off and did whatever the hell you wanted, maybe we wouldn't have to be so goddamned worried!"

"Mom!" I shouted into the phone and it echoed around me. "Mike has absolutely no control over my life anymore, and neither do you. That's the wondrous thing about turning eighteen, freedom. And as for that idiot detective you're so fond of, if I wanted anything to do with him, I would've stayed his little lap dog and not run off the second the opportunity allowed."

"You watch how you talk to me. Do you not see the crowd you've begun to follow?"

I scoffed, feeling like I was in high school all over again. I glanced up the street to the gaggle of oddly dressed vampire folk I was walking behind. Following. I followed just like Mom had accused.

I sighed. "Yeah. I gotta go."

"Please just think before you make stupid choices. Mike and I only want you to be safe. Because we love you and couldn't imagine life without you."

"Mom, Mike already has a life without me. He should be fine with it by now." The other line stayed quiet. "I love you, Mom." I hung up without waiting to hear what else she had to say. Whatever it may have been probably would've just pissed me off anyway.

"Everything okay?" Cyrus, who'd been walking a respectful distance ahead of me since I'd answered the phone, slowed and asked in a caring tone.

"Yeah," I smiled. "I gotta make a call. I'll catch up."

The pretty man nodded and quickened his pace.

My eyes narrowed in disdain as I dialed. I slowed down and let my three-inch heels take a break.

"This is Mike."

Ugh!!

"Stop talking to my mom," I hissed.

"I didn't realize I was." Once a smartass, always a smartass.

"You know what I mean."

"She called me. What'd you want me to do? Ignore the poor old girl?" I could practically hear his shrug.

"Poor old girl? Didn't my mom kick your ass in beer pong at my birthday party a few months ago?" True story.

"Ha, yeah." He actually sounded a bit sheepish.

"You've got her worried sick!" I nearly screeched.

"The five o'clock news had her scared. They finally started reporting this story after a few of the cases came together. I calmed her down. She called me asking if I'd go with her to the airport to come get you. I let her know I'd already talked to you and filled you in. You're an adult who can make her own decisions." The bastard was just being facetious.

"You're right. I am an adult. I'm an adult on vacation with my friends." The word friends sounded stupid even as I said it. The only friend I had was Tatum, and even she was quickly approaching my shit list. "I'm trying to have fun and get a better understanding of this culture."

"Culture? Just three months ago, you were a jaded bitch, cursing the name of many of those fucking idiots. And now, it's culture? And what happened to the research? Hardcore journalist on the hunt for a killer story? Nope. You're out for understanding." His deep voice lowered. "Why don't you just fuck him already?"

A shrill scoff flew from my throat before I could control it. The ridiculous comment, no matter how true it may have been, actually hurt my feelings. As if I was some kind of slut.

"What's to say I haven't?" I let those words sting as best I could. "Haven't you learned by now not to challenge me? You'll always lose in that department. Because, in the end, you have zero control of what I do."

He didn't say anything for a long time. I knew I'd hurt him. And really, I kind of felt bad. But he should have known better. I didn't do well with challenges and ultimatums. I liked to have it my way and rarely gave in to the will of others. Unless of course, the other was walking a few feet ahead of me in a sexy midnight-black suit, tailored to fit his unworldly body.

"I know," he said finally. His voice cracked as if he was trying not to cry and I instantly felt terrible.

No matter how much Mike annoyed the shit out of me, I really did love him. I couldn't stand him. I couldn't date him. And I sure as hell couldn't live with him, but it didn't mean I wanted him to hurt. Especially not on my account.

"I'm fine. I know who I'm dealing with. I know how dangerous people can be."

"These people." I heard him swallow hard. Knowing him, he was swallowing his pain.

"No. People. All people," I rebutted.

"If you need anything, call me."

"You mean if I *know* anything, call you." I made it a statement because I already knew it to be true. It didn't matter how much Detective Michael Petersen said he loved me, he was always after the bottom line. And in this case, the bottom line was a shitload of missing heads. We were more alike than I liked to admit.

"Sure." He hung up without another word.

Hanging up angrily on a cell phone, with only a little button on a screen, is nowhere near as effective as the old-fashioned receiver being slammed into the base. There was always a little aftershock from that. Like you got to hear the ringer clang from the force of it. On both ends, much more satisfying. Damn technology.

I was damned irritated and fairly certain my mother and Michael Petersen were gabbing on the phone about how much trouble I was getting myself in to. Apparently, it never dawned on either of them that their precious Dylan was well over twenty-one years old and perfectly capable of handling herself. Mike always got my mom in an uproar. It had only gotten worse since the whole "Dylan killed two vampire boys thing. Granted, that was pretty scary, but he didn't have to tell my mom *everything*. I'd saved his fucking life for God's sake. I may have also shot Cyrus in the process, but I did the best I could under the circumstances. Shit, I should've gotten a medal. I should've been counting my lucky stars I wasn't locked away up in Chowchilla with the other murderesses of California. But all that should go to show I could take care of myself. Mostly.

And Mike comes in handy in a legal pinch.

Shut up.

Cyrus had turned to see if I was keeping up and I gave him an innocent grin. He waited for me to catch up. I teetered uncomfortably on heels I should have left at home, and the two of us walked together, separated by a good fifty feet from the rest of the crowd.

"Should we catch up?" I asked, concerned we might get lost without the others to lead the way. "Wouldn't wanna get lost out here." As if we were wandering around in the open wilderness or something.

"I know the way." He looked straight ahead as if seeing things in his head that I was deliberately unaware of. "Been the same for a long time. Not far now." I was glad to hear that. My feet were killing me and I didn't want to be a pain in the ass and ask to stop so I could change my shoes again.

With the others so far ahead, I decided to use my alone time wisely. "So, Secondus, eh?" I left it at that. If he chose to answer, it was up to him.

"Yes." No emotion.

"And this is a secret?" I asked jokingly.

"Not something I care to tell the world."

"Isn't it like a big deal? To be the second in command?" I tried to keep my tone light and not allow my previous bullshit conversation to seep in. I wanted two things from him, and neither would be attained with force. They *could* have been, but I had to leave my gun at home.

"I believe you have the wrong idea."

"So, explain it to me." Silence. "I promise, off the record."

After a few breaths, he began. "Secondus is not a prestigious title in the House of Cailleadh. Some Houses revere their Secondus as they do their Primus. Malcolm prefers I not become a spectacle," his voice remained monotone. It reminded me of the way he spoke to me the first time we'd met after I'd asked him about where he'd come from. When he'd told me he was Persian in his Cy-bot tone.

"So instead you prance around in your man panties and pose for the cameras? That sounds legit." Sarcasm flowed from my lips without filtration. As per usual.

"He feels that is his best use for me," he said with little inflection.

"Why don't you leave? I mean, he's just a person, what's he gonna do to you?" I caught myself before saying, "cut your head off?" Seemed a bit too soon.

"That's not how it works," he said as he shook his head.

"He's holding you captive? Explain it to me really, because I'm not understanding how a man, such as yourself, can be so submissive to a little red-haired weasel like McTavish? Seems a bit ridiculous to me."

"You don't like to be submissive, do you?" His tone made the question dirty, I blushed with sexual tension, and didn't appreciate the innuendo.

"No, I don't. But we aren't talking about me. We're talking about you. You and that asshole Malcolm. Why are you any part of all this in the first place? What the fuck do you get out of it? You obviously have no interest in the scene. So, why?" I stopped in my tracks, folded my arms across my chest, and waited for his answer.

His warm hands slid up my arms giving me the chills and causing a serious case of goose bumps. "Never mind all that." A terrifying grin spread across his lips. Terrifying with its implications of danger and other things. "Here we are." His perfect green eyes left my gaze and glanced up at a towering old warehouse.

Towering over us at three stories tall, the old brick building held a huge canvas banner. Painted across it in scrolling letters was Endless Night Masque de Sang, and a pair of fangs beside the last word. Blazing from the roof, two spotlights spun in the sky like two long reaching light sabers in a dueling battle. The group we'd been trailing behind had all but disappeared into the grand double door entrance and dozens more filed in. Crowding the street and sidewalk, hundreds of little Goth kids mingled about puffing on stinking cigarettes and trying to look as ominous as possible. Some reminded me of Philippe, so pathetically hopeless. Others seemed as though they were right where they belonged.

Masks, wings, Victorian dresses, steampunk inspired ensembles, and everything in between flittered about, excited for the party to come. From what I gathered, the doors were only open to certain guests, and the others were forced to wait out front.

"Are you ready?" Cyrus asked, pulling me by my arm toward the doors.

"Can we get in?" I replied, looking around at the ever-growing crowd of misfit vampires.

A soft laugh escaped his throat. "We are the elite." He pulled from his pocket a rectangular ticket with VIP written in white on the top. Other words were scrawled beautifully along its shiny surface, but I couldn't make them out in the darkness.

A red velvet rope stood between the party and the two of us, but it seemed those two pieces of shiny square paper were our ticket in. I'd never really thought I'd need a ticket. Figured the huge red head would work his Primus mojo and get us in.

"You'll need this," he reached into his inner jacket pocket and pulled out a black lace mask. "May I?" he asked, holding it up.

Confused, I turned my back to him to allow him to tie it up. Gently, he placed the intricate lace over my eyes and tied the long black ribbon at the back of my head. In all my preparation, I hadn't even considered I'd need a mask for the masque. I'd have failed at Boy Scouting.

Mask in place, I felt silly, but when I turned back around, Cyrus was pulling a manlier version from his pocket. He quickly tied the black leather mask around his head with its straps. I noticed then he and I matched almost entirely. His black on black three-piece suit had silk ribbing along the cuffs and lapel matching the hem of my tea-length black dress. The plunging square neckline of my dress and the thin straps were also of the same silk. Normally, intentional match-y-match would've driven me insane, but ours was in no way a planned coordination. Besides, the evening seemed to warrant such foolishness so I decided to roll with it. If I were stuck having match someone, it might as well have been Cyrus Atossa.

Prepared for my first ever vampire masquerade, I waited like a good little reporter for the man at the door to move the pointless red velvet rope so we could enter. The rope dropped to the floor and Cyrus led us into the first real vampire event of the Halloween weekend. I really was about to spend an evening in a warehouse filled with nasty little blood drinkers.

And me without my camera.

EIGHT

THE SPACE INSIDE WAS HUGE, A VAST WAREHOUSE INDEED. It looked nothing like a warehouse anymore. Long white drapes were suspended from metal beams that ran along the high industrial ceiling. Each a few yards wide, hung from the ceiling to floor. The red lighting made the white of the fabric appear pink and shadowed in shades of red. The drapes hung at random intervals throughout the space, forcing the guests to weave through them. The effect lent mystique to the extra-large space, adding a sense of intimacy and a slightly uneasy feeling from the lack of open space. In any other setting, I would've liked the look of it, very Cirque du Soleil, but in a room full of people who may or may not want to have me for dinner, I was on the ready for something gory to happen.

The floor was done in a black and white checkered pattern

that covered the entire space. Again, the red light caused the white of the tile to appear a deep shade of pink. A large stage encompassed the length of the far wall. To the left was a bar and my first stop. I'd expected there'd be more patrons than what there were, but I assumed we were a bit early judging by the gaggle of vampire folk congregating outside. I started walking toward the bar, which was not as packed as I thought it'd be, but was stopped by a hand on my shoulder.

"My sweet girl, we don't drink here. This… space… is for them." Malcolm released my shoulder and flipped his fingers toward the crowd that had started to gather at the front entrance.

Surprisingly, McTavish appeared to treat me as an equal. Sort of. He spoke to me in a normal tone using normal words. It was a start. I wasn't buying it.

"Um, okay. Then please direct me to the 'white's only drinking fountain.'" Yes, air quotes. And, yes, a fucking joke.

He smiled at me, and my heart sank an inch in my chest. The look in his eyes was the look a cat gets when it's about to claw the shit out of your face.

A heavy base drum hit from nowhere, breaking my concentration, and the lights changed in an instant from red to blue. Suddenly, the long drapes that hung so elegantly from the ceiling became home to mostly nude women. Each of the dozen or so strips of white fabric was suddenly adorned with a topless girl. Simultaneously, they slid down their drape, clinging with one leg and one hand. For a second time, a base drum beat; the girls released their grip and fell backward. Upside down they slid until they were halfway down the sheet. I stood only a handful of feet away from a lovely brunette. She trailed down the cloth, getting closer to the floor below her. Closer to me. I could see her face as she drew nearer to the end of her rope. She was beautiful. Her face was soft and delicate and held not an ounce of fear sliding twenty-five-feet upside down, clinging to a piece of cloth with only her leg. She was above me only a few feet when she smiled. Blue light glinted off her remarkable eyes. They looked like the sea at night. Glistening in waves of light and shadow. I held her gaze steadfast as she descended. An intricate dragon tattoo wrapped around her waist and up her bare chest. She was so close I could almost touch her, and a part of me wanted to. There was a kind of primal sexual heat radiating off the naked girl hanging from the cloth.

Just as quickly as it happened the first time, the music began with another drum beat, and the girls lifted themselves upright and began climbing back up the fabric. Wrapping hands and legs around the silky, flowing fabric, each girl maneuvered themselves upward. Our eye contact broke, and she was gone, back up her curtain, and I was left standing there like a lovesick school girl. Only, I had no idea who she was or why in the hell I had any interest in her.

I can appreciate a pretty girl when I see one, but never in my life have I been so intrigued by a woman.

The girls continued their dance on the curtains. They wrapped themselves in the long fabric, flipped and turned, and slid. It was an awe provoking dance. The agility and fearlessness those girls had baffled me. Granted I'd killed people, but that was nothing compared to plummeting to your death half naked in front of a crowd of people dressed like they were on their way to a macabre renaissance fair.

"Dylan, let's go," Tatum called to me from a few feet away. She and Malcolm made their way toward a set of spiraling stairs hidden in a dark corner. Cyrus waited cordially for my attention.

The man in black stuck his arm out for me, but I ignored it. I let my ass wiggle back and forth as my disgustingly tall heels hit the tile floor with a stomp. I wanted to stay and watch the girls wrap and hang. I made sure to calm myself before I hit the expanded metal staircase. A spiked heel meets a holey surface and a girl could be done for.

Tatum and Malcolm had almost disappeared up the stairs by the time I reached the foot of it. I forced myself to slowly take it one step at a time. I tried to ignore the sudden fear that crept up my spine knowing I was by myself, even if only for a minute, in a room full of blood drinkers. No matter how fictional they were, drinking someone's blood was no bullshit.

I felt Cyrus at my back after a few steps up the stairs. The music was so loud there was no hearing someone sneak up on you, but after so many years spent in a bar, I'd grown accustomed to not being able to hear myself speak let alone anyone else.

Perched atop the treacherous stairs was a loft area that stretched the length of the room and jutted from the brick wall a few dozen feet over the floor below. A large man stood at the entrance to the area stopping all who should attempt to cross the line. He stopped me with an open hand at my chest. I scoffed before I realized he'd never hear it, and then I pointed at Malcolm's fiery red mane. Cyrus came up behind me, and the man moved aside to let us through. I couldn't resist and I made a childish face of victory at the dumb guy on the stairs. For once in my life, I was with the in-crowd.

Blood drinkers or not, they sure as hell know how to party.

Huge lounge chairs and sectional sofas sat sporadically throughout the open area, each a different color. Some blue, some red, some black, but all overstuffed and made for beauty as well as comfort. Small cube shaped tables sat in front of each seating area and allowed a place for drinks or butts. Gorgeous people lounged on every available spot. Some lounged on another person, but no one seemed to mind the closeness.

The upper deck, as I'd dubbed it in my own head, seemed a far cry from the mundane open floor below. It appeared as though they grouped all the beautiful people up the stairs of death where the big couches were and all the idiots in ruffled shirts and top hats were forced to mingle below. Such as peasants or peons maybe. It reminded me of Diego, or Philippe, pathetic little boys in the presence of less pathetic little boys. Everyone in the room, to the general public, would seem as just another Goth kid with low self-esteem and a mommy complex, but amongst themselves, they were incredible creatures. They had their own hierarchy and set of rules in place that didn't touch the world I lived in, the real world. But it worked for them. Someone like Malcolm, a pale redheaded boy with freckles who thought himself a vampire would have been teased mercilessly in high school. Even as an adult, in a crowd made up of Billy-Bobs, he'd be eaten alive. In fact, I couldn't believe these people didn't get more grief than they did. *If* they did. I had to say, it felt nice not being on the floor with the commoners. Even if I was surrounded by the head honchos of the vampire club.

The four of us made our way through the crowd that took up the upper deck, toward a black couch in the shape of a half-circle. It was all the way in the back, stuck in a corner, but it was the only available spot.

"Nobody puts Baby in the corner," I quipped. "Why are we all the way back here? You can't work your Primus mojo and get us a better seat?" I wasn't trying to complain, honest.

"This *is* the better seat. This is the spot I choose every year.

It has the best view and is the farthest away from gawkers and sheep." Malcolm acted as though he was so far above me and everyone else in the room he couldn't stand to be near us.

Letting out an irritated and totally childish sigh, I plopped unattractively on the big comfy couch. Malcolm rolled his eyes in disgust, as I knew he would, and I smiled sweetly at him. He was right, the view was spectacular. I could see the stage, the bar, all of the drapery girls, and all of the peons below.

I glanced around the upper deck and noticed the group sitting within the seating area next to us. Two women and a man, all looking like they could be related to Cyrus with their pouty lips and thick eyelashes. The man wore a top hat and mask, done up in simple black silk. The red-haired woman donned a dress that made me want to run to a costume shop and buy anything other than the plain black dress I had on. The shoulders were covered in shiny black feathers that trailed down the long sleeves and up her neck to create a high collar that circled her head. Her milk white skin was like Malcolm's, but she pulled it off better. A woman with jet-black hair sat with them in a black leather dress that reminded me of Edward Scissorhands with all of its buckles and straps. Her eyes met mine and reflected the light emanating from the lower level in a way that reminded me of my first night with Cyrus. Glowing, almost as though they produced their own light, in a way so unnatural it seemed computer generated.

I've got to find out where they get those contacts.

One of the women, the redhead, raised a bulbous, stemmed glass to me with a nod of her head and drank. The thick liquid in the glass stuck to the edges as it tipped up and back down. It looked like syrup or oil… or blood. My breath caught and I let out a tiny gasp. I knew where I was. I knew who they were and what they thought they were. I just never thought that I'd ever see someone drinking blood from a wine glass only a few feet from me.

"You know what they are, Dylan, darling." Cyrus spoke closely to my ear. I felt his breath roll across the skin of my neck and shivered when it sent chills down my spine.

I know what they think *they are. Sometimes, when I'm alone and drunk in my apartment, I think I'm Joan Jett. Do I flaunt that in public? Nope.*

"Yes. It was just unexpected. That *is* what I think it is, right?" I knew what it was. What else could it be?

"Yes. Willing donors only, love," Malcolm's Irish brogue chimed in with an answer. "Every year a select group of donors is given a free pass to the event in exchange for their… donation. What you see there was collected days ago and chilled for the occasion. Be prepared, that's not the first or the last. Masque de Sang has been celebrated for years without instance . It won't change now. I would suggest you order yourself a drink and try to have fun." He smiled at me for the fifth time since I'd met him. Either he was actually trying to be civil with me for Tatum's sake, or he was secretly planning my gory death and didn't want me to catch on.

A scantily clad waitress shimmied over to our group with a tray in hand. Her hair was ratted up into a twist over her head that looked straight out of a Tim Burton movie. Smudged black makeup under her eyes made it look like she'd been crying. The overall look was scary, but I loved it. I ordered and she flashed a fanged smile at me. I laughed nervously, and she winked at me.

"You know, Maxwell is fitting custom teeth at his booth tonight. We should get a pair." Cyrus smiled too and I pictured him with his shiny white fangs from my dream so many months ago. A quick battle of emotions occurred in my head as I struggled over whether the idea was terrifying or sexy.

"We, as in you and I?" Sexy won.

"Oh, I want to go too." Tatum piped up from the other side of Malcolm. She'd been uncharacteristically quiet for so long I'd forgotten she was there. Which was not entirely a bad thing. She still hadn't acknowledged the fact she was shackled permanently to her Sanguinarian candy cane boyfriend, or that I'd finally said it in public, to more than just her.

"Let me get a few drinks in me, and we'll see," I said with a fake smile. I fought hard not to scream. To grab her by her stupid blonde face and tell her she was acting like a lovesick fool. It wasn't like her to fall all over herself for some guy, and why the first time it happens it was with Ginger Spice, I'd never know.

Maybe it's some kind of vampire power. He's got Cyrus in his clutches... why not drag Tatum along too? Vampire mind control....

"Is that all it takes?" Cyrus butted into my thoughts and startled me back to reality. Shooting me a wink that washed thoughts of Tatum away, he replaced them with naughty thoughts, and my weekend immediately became much better. A sly wink from the silly vampire boy and I melted in my control-top panties. While Tatum ruffled my feathers, Cyrus was right behind her to smooth them down again. "A few drinks?"

"Usually." I winked right back. The conversation was heading in a direction that caused serious turmoil in my little head. On the one hand, Cyrus had driven me absolutely insane until the last six hours. But on the other hand, sexual frustration was a nasty bitch.

Our drinks arrived, and I sent mine careening down my gullet almost immediately. Awkward situations were better handled intoxicated. Really, it was true. Ordering another drink, okay two, I secretly hoped I'd get drunk and lose all inhibitions. I knew I was my own worst enemy and tended to cut off my dick to spite my balls. Also, likely the sole reason for my recent celibacy. Somewhere in my head, the thought lingered that it might be the night to rectify my dry spell.

Planning on adding that to your book?

Sex sells, baby.

Allowing myself to relax and enjoy the situation, I leaned against the cushioned back of the low-profile couch. My eyes closed lazily and my mind began to take in the music thumping in my ears. Low bellowing drum beats as there had been when the girls made their descent from the ceiling, but now there were other instruments added and a woman's soprano vocals. The small amount of alcohol I'd consumed found a home in my stomach, making it warm with its fiery liquid. I opened curious eyes and focused on the crowd below. Specifically the girls dangling precariously from the steel rafters on those fancy drapes. Each stretched and curled their strong limbs around the silky fabric. Legs and arms, winding and curling their way up, up, up. Then, without the slightest hesitation, they fell. Legs wrapped intricately around the cloth. The synchronization was intermittent, but I wondered if that was also choreographed.

I'd been inside the building for just under twenty minutes, and I was already sucked into the romance of it all. The fearlessness of the women suspended from the ceiling. Even those in the top hats and capes had courage to let their freak flag fly. I noticed then how easy it must've been to attract newbies. I, as a strong-willed adult, knew this was not the lifestyle for me and I had no intention of carrying on the façade beyond the weekend. But, if I were some lonely neglected teenager, that moment would've been the moment I accepted all of that shit as my new life. Luckily for me, I was not lonely or neglected, or a teenager. Well, I wasn't a teenager.

The skinny waitress returned with a tray full of clear shot glasses filled with thick red liquid. Hesitant, I held one of my shots a foot or so away from my face and examined the contents. On any other day, if someone were to hand me a red-liquid filled glass the first thing on my mind would not have been, hey is this blood? But, when in Rome. Or, Transylvania….

"What is this?" I asked, taking a sniff of the contents.

"Not what you think it is. What would a vampire party be without bloody good drinks?" Malcolm laughed a full belly laugh. It was the first time I'd ever even seen him smile more than a simple grin. I never noticed his set of fangs before. They were kind of dainty and slightly hidden by his upper lip. It was a little bit of a relief to know he had some kind of human emotion, but the relief was halted when I caught a glimpse of those pointy things in his mouth. Primus or not, Malcolm did not seem the type to indulge in the dramatics of his culture. I always saw him as a businessman, not a vampire fashionista.

Everyone in my group raised their matching shots in a silent toast. The four of us slung our drinks back and slammed them down damn near simultaneously. I laughed at the action and the others followed. Tatum's laugh was a refreshing sound I hadn't had the pleasure of in quite a while. Not saying she didn't laugh, just that she and I hadn't laughed together for some time and I missed that. I missed her. It didn't matter what I said to her.

I figured then that I might as well forget trying to control the events of the weekend and just go with it. I told myself I'd learn more about their culture by being a part of it than observing it from the outside. Maybe I could even start to understand the odd relationship Tatum had going with Malcolm. Or not. Either way, short of boarding the next flight home, that was my life for the following few days. I figured I may as well make the best of it. Besides, Tatum had Malcolm, I might as well have Cyrus. Even if just for the weekend.

Oh hell, I guess so.

Alright, I was very much in the mood to have fun and the environment warranted specifically that. So I decided to let my bitch slide for the evening, sue me.

"How 'bout those fangs?" I smiled slyly.

Cyrus smiled, and his pearly whites glimmered in the dim light. "Are you ready then?"

"As long as I can take them out in the morning… what the hell."

"Thank God," he let out a relieved exhale.

"What?"

"I was terrified you were about to say YOLO," Cyrus said with the utmost seriousness.

I laughed as hard and as loud as was unattractive. Stopping just before a fart slipped out, I let out a heavy sigh of suspended laughter.

"I don't think anything could have appeared odder than watching a big tough vampire boy use the phrase YOLO. Not to mention how incredibly endearing it is that you were relieved I didn't say it. Trust me, sitting in the VIP section of the plastic fang club is neither the time nor the place for a You Only Live Once moment. They might prove me wrong." My laughter started again but stopped when I saw the look on Cyrus's face. A light smirk lingered on my warm and tingly cheeks. The alcohol was beginning to sink in to each cell of my body. A thought ran through my head, and I worried maybe the drinks were spiked as they had been at Embrace.

"I'm not a vampire boy." His expression told me he was dead serious.

"Well then, what else would you call the Secondus of the House of Malcolm's bitch?" I was starting to feel a bit snotty.

"House of Cailleadh. And just because I'm Secondus does not make me the same as those… people," his eyes shot toward the dance floor below with disdain.

"Then why do you do it?" I asked, taking the chance to look him dead in the eye.

His gaze shifted to look at Malcolm sitting to his left on the rounded couch. I continued to watch him, trying to decipher his body language. It was obvious he was checking on Malcolm, but he gave nothing else away. After a few long moments of silence, I let it go. I assumed he wouldn't talk with Malcolm so close, and though Malcolm was stuck up Tatum's ass, it appeared as though Cyrus was afraid he might overhear. I could care less who heard what, but then again, I wasn't stuck with the guy day in and day out. Or was that night in and night out?

"Fine. I need a drink," I said, short and to the point. I crossed one leg over the other and let my back relax into the soft cushion.

Cyrus lifted his hand and waved his fingers around at someone I didn't really see at the stair-end of the long loft area. Kind of annoyed, with Malcolm, again, for no obvious reason other than his presence, I chose to ignore the crew and stare at the crowd writhing on the dance floor below. Each in their own getup, sporting their own rendition of what a vampy looked like, looking like they'd just passed through the gates of their own heaven. Or wherever little vampire kids dream of being. Oh,

New Orleans. Made sense.

"You promised dancing," I said to Cyrus without taking my eyes off the lower level.

"Would that make you happy?" His hand grazed mine and thc hcat madc mc jump.

An inner ironic snicker ran through my thoughts, for a little vampire boy, he sure was warm. "Does it really matter to you what makes me happy?" I let the snicker slide from my lips.

"Actually, yes," he said like it surprised him too. "You intrigue me, Dylan Hart. You are unlike any other girl I've met in my life."

"Thanks. But I've heard that before. And trust me, it'll pass. Eventually you'll realize it's really not that fun. Soon enough you'll see. I'm a novelty, honey. You'll love to play with me for a short time, then you'll realize how much I am *not* what you're looking for." I never took my eyes off the floor below as I recited the spiel I had so many times before. So far, the only person who ignored it with vigor was Mike. Even then, it didn't work out.

"We'll see." His resolve seemed strong, but I didn't buy it. He was pretty enough and sweet when he wanted to be, but a relationship with Dylan Hart was a long row to hoe and I'd just as soon not put anyone through that torture. Besides, I just wanted to sleep with him.

The pretty girl with the fucked-up makeup was back and standing exquisitely in front of me. She carried her silver tray with a multitude of glasses perched atop its shiny surface. Expecting her to hand me one drink, I held my hand out, but instead, she sat the entire tray on the small circular table situated in the center of our group. She had brought us, four people, twelve enticing alcoholic beverages. A few seemed a bit odd in color and texture, but I figured they were part of the experience.

YOLO.

Oh, fuck no.

Just kidding.

Malcolm reached his pale hand out and snagged one of the interesting glasses as I was about to grab it. He handed it to Tatum and grabbed another for himself before I had a chance to choose one. I vowed to myself to make a serious attempt at kicking that man square in the nuts before the weekend was over. Just because. The glasses were of the tumbler variety and thus likely a mixed drink of some kind. Not really my style anyway. As if reading my mind, for the millionth time in recent history, Cyrus nabbed one of the tall shot glasses filled with a sickly intoxicating substance, and handed it to me. Taking one for himself, he lifted it to toast.

I squished my brows together in inquiry. "Are we toasting to something?"

"Yes. A toast to… connection." He tilted his glass to his lips.

"What?" I responded with a stupid tone to my voice.

"Connection. We rarely have had the chance for much contact and I'd like that to change."

"Like, you're gonna send me a friend request on Facebook? I'm not really following along here." It was awkward not knowing what the fuck he was talking about.

He smiled sweetly, "No, darling, a connection, the type of contact you have outside of the Internet. Such as eye contact."

His brows rose indicating he noticed my general lack of meeting his eyes. I had a good reason dammit. His eyes made it hard for me to focus on, well, anything. And that wasn't a power I wanted to give over to anyone. "Such as physical contact." His heavy hand ran across my forearm, and I held my breath.

I worried I was becoming soft. I worried his charms would win me over. I worried I'd get drunk and sleep with him and it'd be horrible. I really worried my arms were hairy. He laughed a little and I let the breath out.

Dylan, I told myself, I often called myself by name, *Dylan*, I thought, *get your shit in check. Get it in check or this little vampire boy is going to run right over you. Maybe he'll be naked when he does it.* A smirk snuck in and I decided I was not a good person to talk to at that point. Not a good advice giver. Nope.

I looked to Tatum and promptly looked away. Her idiot vampire boy had his ginger kid face buried in her neck. I told myself he was just hooking her up with a disgusting hickey and left it at that. I hated to think of her allowing that freak to sink teeth in and draw blood. The memory of her slicing into my skin when she had cut me open and licked blood from the wound in a vamp den in Fresno made my stomach churn. All was fine and good until someone drew blood… and drank it.

"A dance?" Cyrus broke my thoughts at just the right moment. Just before I allowed my head to take over and tell me what a stupid mistake I was making being involved in this bloody mess.

"You got it, kid." I stood on wobbly legs and waited a moment for them to settle. The first few steps after a good round of drinks kind of reminded me of a baby calf minutes after birth.

Cyrus led me by the hand down the length of the loft and toward the burly man at the head of the stairs. The man gave a nod and a wink, but surprisingly enough it was not aimed at the man in the lead. It was intended for me. I smiled back, acknowledging I understood his innuendo, and planned on getting very drunk and very naked and was damn proud of it.

Hand in hand, the two of us, alone for the first time in quite a few months, weaved through the droves of winged and masked vampire people flailing and writhing along the checkered floor. The girls on the drapes had gone away leaving their long silky strands to dangle alone in sporadic intervals throughout the space. Cyrus pulled me through the crowd, allowing the long white drapes to slide over his head and shoulders, falling across my face and tickling along my bare skin. Lights flashed and pulsated in color. Sweat and blood filled the air. People touched my body as I passed them, each sensation new and intriguing. I smiled wildly on my journey across the dance floor, thoroughly enjoying the experience more than I should have. For a girl who didn't want to get on that plane in the first place, I sure as fuck was glad I had. At that moment, anyway.

Cyrus stopped and turned to face me; his façade more open than I'd ever seen it. Striking green eyes peered from behind his black leather mask. Away from Malcolm, comfortable with his newly found confidante, and likely a little tipsy, Cyrus suddenly became accessible. As though he was an actual person, unlike the perfect shell of a human I'd always assumed him to be.

I tried to be as smooth as I possibly could. Letting the music fill my head with its electric beat, I allowed my body to do the rest. Not the best plan, but I didn't really have much else in my repertoire, so I went with it. The crowd danced rhythmically with the feminine vocals. We started out a few feet apart from each other. My body moved separately from his in mostly an uncoordinated wiggle. After a few moments of that idiocy, he placed his hands on either side of my waist and drew my wiggling body closer to his. I hadn't had quite enough alcohol to not feel awkward, so I had to fake it. And fake it I did.

Cyrus's rhythm was easy to fall into. His motion brought the music to the forefront in my head. His body made me forget my insecurities, and I began to allow myself to just be. Just be in the moment. Just let shit happen as it may. And it did.

Cyrus pressed the front of his chiseled form against my full chest, and I felt my boobs push up and around looking for a place to go. His hands slid smoothly around to my lower back and stayed there. The heat of his breath tickled along the tender skin of my neck, and I nearly fell out of my ass. I quickly reminded myself to never allow that long of a dry spell to occur again and moved on.

He stood a good head taller than me, but my heels gave me a bit of an advantage and placed his pouty lips within kissing distance. I thought about it more than once as our bodies were pressed so closely together dancing to intentionally sensual music. His smooth cheek touched mine. My heart raced with the idea of kissing that perfect set of lips held so beautifully on his face.

The beat thumped on and with it the two of us. The strong muscles that lined Cyrus's arms, flexed and relaxed as he moved against me. I let my hands trail along the expanse of his thick back and felt the tension there as well. For the first time in a long time, I allowed myself to breathe in his luscious scent. He smelled so clean and masculine I wanted to gobble him up. I felt his heartbeat quicken as he breathed heavily in my ear. The action was far from his usual calm and collected demeanor, but it made him more reachable somehow. More human. I knew it was coming. I could feel it. A spark touched my senses and I knew he was making up his mind to grant me a kiss. Cyrus lowered his head to rest his cheek along the curve of my neck.

The lace of my mask caressed the soft skin under my eyes and reminded me of its presence. The two of us, masked, dancing, pressed closely together, surrounded by danger, someone would pay good money to read a book that began in such a way. I wondered if the ending would live up to such a glorious beginning.

I smiled a bit and waited in sweet anticipation. His breath came heavier and more rapid with every passing second. I shifted my head ever so slightly to allow my hair to brush against his face still hidden in my neck. He drew back from me enough to make our lips close enough to kiss. Closing my eyes, I prepared for awesomeness. His breath spread across my face and I knew it was coming. I wanted it, really. I hadn't really any other time I'd been in his presence, but at that moment I knew I didn't quite care about much else. Not much on my thoughts, but laying a smooch on Cyrus Atossa. His lips neared mine, and I lifted myself up on my toes to meet him. The aura of his lips mingled with my own.

"And now!" a boisterous voice echoed through the vast

industrial building.

Cyrus quickly withdrew from his position, only centimeters from meeting my lips for the first time.

Universe, you're a fickle bitch.

NINE

HE TURNED HIS HEAD TO FOCUS ON THE STAGE. HIS BREATHING was steadying, but I felt his tension remain. Muscles in his jaw flexed in the shimmering light from the stage and I knew he was clenching it in concentration.

"For your viewing pleasure, I present to you, Madam Azelie. The snake charmer." The large bellied man on stage bowed and held his hand out with a flourish, welcoming the performer to the stage.

The little woman took the stage with such presence I hardly believed there was just one small human being exuding that much confidence . My favorite Cajun voodoo priestess entered stage left with a bigass snake draped around her petite form.

Just fucking fantastic!

Serious pyrotechnics ignited on either side of the stage

and silence fell over the crowd. A moment later, the rhythmic beat of a drum began. The woman's hips swayed with an ease you rarely saw in reality. Something more cat-like than human movement. Her hands rose and lifted each end of the snake with them. The multilayered skirt that clung to her hips swished with her movement. Back and forth it swayed, exposing bare legs and feet through its shorter layers. Around her midsection, an interesting tattoo wrapped around and nearly met at her belly button. The skirt hit at her hips, hardly covering her crotch, hanging so low I feared it might fall off. Her body continued its undulation, and I grew even more annoyed by the little bitch. Not only had she all but strung me up by my neck in her tiny witch room, she was distracting my pseudo date from his thoughts of kissing me. I decided two things then, first, that bitch was on my list, and second, I was going to kiss those perfect fucking lips if I had to tie the boy down to do it. I might just tie him down anyway.

A woman passed, carrying a tray of drinks, and I swiped two. One slid down the hatch and the other waited its turn in my trembling hand. I never understood why he showed me the slightest bit of interest. Why he'd ever wasted his time on a fatty like me, I didn't know. When I first met Cyrus, I thought he was full of shit, hell maybe he still was, but I was at the point I didn't really care. He was pretty and I wanted him. End of story.

I waited a good thirty seconds before I shoved the glass on deck to my lips. The hot liquid slid over my tongue and burned my throat on the way down. My eyes closed from the sensation and a shiver shook my core. Cyrus watched the woman on stage and I watched him. Though his eyes were fixed on her, they didn't appear to hold a sense of longing or attraction. I thought, for a second, I saw fear. Just a second and it was gone. It reminded me of the time he'd been so scared of Dominika. The thought of *that* crazy bitch pissed me off even more. Luckily for me, she wasn't staying in that house with us, but I was sure she was in attendance nonetheless. That was the last thing I wanted to deal with.

The woman on stage lifted the snake off her shoulders and allowed it to wrap itself around her waist. The snake was nearly all white, apart from a few splotches of yellow. Likely a python of some kind. I wasn't a snake fan so I didn't really know. It was scaly and had no legs; it was a fucking snake.

Her costume was revealing, hardly covering her nipples, allowing the world to see she was covered in simple black-line tattoos; naked arms showed off bands of inked designs from wrist to shoulder. The hip hugging skirt coupled with the mesh string bikini style top left little to the imagination. On the forefront, for all to see, the tiny girl bore markings of ink on her body that resembled those on her lovely sign hanging in front of her shop of bullshit. I'd had the pleasure of seeing most of those tattoos up close and personal, but even if I hadn't, they were obvious against her creamy skin. Dangling from her wrist, right where it'd been when I'd seen her last was her black rosary.

The sight of that woman pissed me off. She really hadn't done anything to me, aside from accuse me of murder, but that was enough to put her on my shit list. I watched her intently as she moved so smoothly with the music and that damn snake. Her thick mane of dreadlocks sat piled in a loose bun on top of her head with bits and pieces sticking out at random.

The flaming columns, which sat on either side of the stage, flamed high and were beginning to heat up the area closest to the stage. Cyrus and I were only about five or six heads back from the thick of it, and I was starting to sweat. Especially under my fancy lace mask Cyrus had so kindly brought along for me. A bead of sweat trickled down my brow, soaking the lace, and dripped onto my eyelash. The salty liquid burned my already irritated eye and it started to twitch uncontrollably. I wiped it as best I could, trying to remain stealthy with the action.

Eye cloudy with sweat, I looked back to the tiny little bitch on the stage and my breath caught in my throat. She was dancing, nothing had changed, but her eyes were focused on me. My eyes grew wide and I stared right back. Experience told me to stand my ground, to stare her down like I had nothing to fear. My intuition told me to get the fuck out of dodge. Keeping my eyes fixed on the woman, Azelie, my hand reached to grab the attention of Cyrus. She stared at me and I stared right back, scared out of my fucking mind.

As quietly and nonthreatening as possible I said, "Cyrus, I think we should leave."

A hand slid around my waist and I felt a slim body press against my back. A sweet scent of woman's perfume wafted into my nose. "But you've only just arrived darling, Donnie," an all too familiar Hungarian voice hissed into my ear.

What is this? Scary bitches 'r' us?

Trying not to take my eyes off the woman on stage, I wriggled my way out of the grip on my waist. "It's Dylan. My fucking name is Dylan," I said through my teeth to the bitch still standing closely behind me. "Dominika, can I help you with something?"

"I should be asking you the same question." Dominika slithered her way between Cyrus and I. She stood between us pointing nonchalantly to the woman on stage. "Seems to me you're the one needing help."

She laughed a raspy, sultry laugh. I wanted so badly to punch her directly in the throat, but I knew better. Dominika needed her ass kicked something fierce and there was no way I was going to be the one to do it. She was a bitch and a fucking scary one at that. Shit, she'd probably pummel my ass into the dirt if she got the chance. Although, watching her interest in the witchy woman on stage gave me an idea. She could pummel someone else just as quickly. An ally, perhaps I should make. And a Yoda moment I will have.

"Yeah, not good," I replied simply.

"How did this happen?" She asked, but she wasn't talking me. She was talking to Cyrus. I was used to it. "How did our darling Donnie get herself on with a priestess?" Her voice held no contempt for me as far as I could tell. It was a first.

"Dylan," Cyrus said plainly.

"My sweet Cyrus," she said as she stroked his thick bicep. "You smell like our girl… *Dylan*. You haven't been snogging a mundane, have you?" She giggled and continued dramatically touching his arm.

"Yes, I have." His eyes remained on the woman. The one who actually mattered at that moment. The fucking scary one. The other scary one. "Dylan decided to visit the priestess. She liked the symbols."

"Lovely," the Hungarian replied as she too stared at the woman on stage.

They both watched the woman watching me. I'd let my eyes slide from the stage to the two beside me and back. As I'd been more than once in the vampire scene, I was fucking clueless and scared out of my ass.

"Well, you two have fun. I am off to find *someone* to eat." Another giggle came from the once mostly terrifying

Hungarian girl.

"Not that I'm complaining," I said still staring at the stage, "but I must say, I'm surprised you are behaving yourself. Honestly, I cringed when I heard your voice in my ear. I have to say, this has been the most pleasant of the few times I've been forced to be in your presence." It was awkward talking to someone I wasn't looking at. Even more awkward telling Dominika I was proud of her good behavior.

"It seems to me you have your hands full with that powerful witch staring a hole in your precious little head." Her long fingernails trailed across the top of my head and down the back of my neck. A shiver tickled my spine. Dominika laid a light kiss on my cheek. "Good luck." She turned and worked her way into the crowd. "Don't let that pretty little girl lose her head now, Cyrus," she called over her shoulder before she disappeared completely.

"So, be honest, why am I getting the stare down from the world's tiniest terror? I have to say she doesn't look scary. Just that horrible tingling feeling I'm getting in the pit of my stomach telling me to run like hell is making me think she might actually be as horrific as she thinks she is."

"Honestly, I'm not completely sure."

"Oh, that's promising. I've somehow—"

Cyrus cut me off. "Well, not somehow, you did kick over her chair and tell her she was fucking nuts."

"Alright, I'll give you that one. But she did accuse me of murder. And does that really give her the motive to intentionally scare the shit out of me?" I'd done worse shit than that in church and you didn't see God coming down and fucking with me, did you? You shouldn't answer that.

"In her world, yes. I would assume she felt threatened and

now she's going to retaliate. It's likely she's just trying to scare you." His words didn't match the tone of uncertainty.

"Or?"

"Or… it's something else."

"Great. Like what?" I asked not really wanting to know the answer.

The girl danced around the flames that had suddenly surrounded the stage. Her body twisted and turned until I could see her full back. It was covered in simple line drawings like those that were scrawled on her sign and all over her body. The drawings that attracted me to her shop in the first place. I wondered why someone would cover their body in tattoos like that and figured she probably had a really good magical mojo reason that I likely did not want to know about. I really did want to know, but knowledge put me that much deeper into the occult. Something told me knowing anything important about those people would put a mark on my head. I was doing well not drowning in headless bitches and vampires without adding voodoo to the mix.

"Nothing. She feels she has power and your display of defiance toward her nicked her ego. She is only trying to show dominance." His brows furrowed and he nodded a teeny tiny bit. It seemed to me like he was trying to convince himself more than me.

"Oh, really?" A sudden rush of adrenaline poured through my limbs at the thought of that tiny girl trying to dominate me. What could she really do to me anyway? She *felt* she had power? That meant shit to me. I didn't do anything to her. She started it.

"Don't get any ideas, Dylan. You'd do well to just leave it alone." His gaze turned to focus on me.

"And let that woman think she can run shit around here?"

"Dylan, aside from Marienne, she *does* run shit around here." He'd been using his big boy potty mouth more than I'd heard from him in the past. I must have been a bad influence.

"You're telling me the only other person who holds as much power as she does is the fucking Primus of the city?" I looked away from the stage to stare at the ever-growing idiot to my right. The idiot nodded and I continued to question his life choices. "So, these people here, in this crowd right now, recognize that woman's power over them?" It was all so unfathomable to me that anyone would accept that as their life.

"Not all, no. But then again not all recognize the power Marienne holds either."

"No one holds anything. Don't you get it? This is America. We are a democracy, a shitty democracy, but a democracy all the same. No one has power over anyone else. You can just walk away. You don't *have* to follow that ginger-headed jar of mayonnaise around like his happy little puppy. And that bitch sure as hell doesn't have any power over *me*." No one held power over me. Ever. I was so against authority I even defied myself sometimes. Yes, I did.

"Dylan, you should probably lower your voice." Cyrus soberly suggested.

"*I* should lower *my* voice? Maybe she should worry about herself and stop trying to throw her 'power' around like she's king shit." Yes, air quotes. "She has power? She can do magic, cast spells, curse me? Let's see it. I don't believe in vampires and I sure as fuck don't believe in magic!"

The crowd was stone silent. The music had stopped. The all-powerful snake charmer on stage was taking her bow. Everyone was looking at me. The snake around her shoulders lifted its huge head and I swear it was looking at me too.

"Shit," I said in a breathless whisper.

"Time to go." Cyrus grabbed me by the hand and pulled me through the crowd.

The scene was eerily familiar to another incident when I'd pissed Dominika off and Cyrus had to drag me away. The incident began with my smart-ass mouth, moved into unknown curses in Hungarian, and turned into me walking in on Tatum sleeping with the enemy. The gingered vamp boy she recently began calling her boyfriend. If history repeated itself, the situation would not end pretty.

My little legs trotted along behind Cyrus as he moved swiftly though the thick crowd of sweaty costume clad vampires, to the stairs that led to the VIP level. I thought we would leave. I figured he'd drag me out the front doors and into the street where he would whisk me away to safety. We ran up the stairs instead of going out the front door.

Had he ever seen a horror movie?

"Where are we going?" I yelled over the sudden beat of industrial music. I didn't receive an answer. "Shouldn't we be leaving?"

"We'll be safer here," his deep voice rumbled.

Cyrus didn't stop for the man at the rope. Without words, the rope was lifted away and we ran through the open space. The overly crowded upper level concealed the two of us as we made our way to Malcolm's prime spot. Our sanctuary. His Primus. Hopefully, being Primus actually gave him some kind of power. I was a hypocrite. I'd admit it. If someone else's belief in power saved my ass, I'd take it. Power to the people.

"There's a problem," Cyrus said, standing in front of a shirtless Primus of the House of Cailleadh.

Malcolm's white skin nearly glowed in the twinkling light from the lower level. I'd never really noticed how ripped he was. I guessed that was the point of a shirt. I didn't question why he had no shirt. *That* was something I really didn't want to know. I stepped around to the other side of Cyrus to get a clear view of the two on the couch. A disgusted sneer lifted my top lip at the sight before me. Malcolm sat, reclined on the circular couch. His white chest was adorned with stark indigo ink of an older tattoo from navel to bulging chest; an intricate Celtic cross took up nearly his entire midsection. Lines of blood sliced across his chest in long bleeding fissures. Tatum, shoeless, sat with her feet curled under her butt, leaning against her half naked boyfriend. She turned her masked face to me and smiled, revealing red stained teeth. I knew what I really hadn't wanted to know. Tatum had been bloodletting. My stomach churned and roiled with the thought of my friend, my confidante, licking the blood from the milky white skin of that asshole. Tatum had officially chosen the dark side, literally, and there was not one damned thing I could do about it. She had dragged me with her to a place of blood and sex with promises of friendship and camaraderie and the only friend I had to my name was the man I'd put a bullet at one point. My friend, Tatum Price, was quickly becoming something I didn't even recognize.

"What is it?" Malcolm asked. His head rolled along the back of the couch and I figured he was drunk. Tatum laid her head on the shoulder of her beau and smiled with drowsy pleasure. They were out of their gourd and likely smashed.

Pack your shit and go home. Run back to your bed. Tuck yourself under that goose down comforter and feel the cold steel of the only fucking thing that will truly be there in a pinch. Drink yourself to oblivion and wait for life to catch up to you.

I met Malcolm's dark green eyes and had to fight with everything I had in me to refrain a serious Chuck Norris roundhouse kick to his Ronald Mc-Goddamned-Donald head. The last thing I wanted was his help.

"Nothing," I answered rudely. The skinny waitress was back with her tray full of liquor goodness. I grabbed two shots and threw one back. "No problem." I slammed the glass back down on her tray and drank the other. "Please, don't stop on our account," I said, using my hands to ensure they understood my words. Well, one hand. One finger to be exact.

I let my ass flop down on the couch. My knees pressed together, my feet lazily held my legs in a modest position. I rested my elbows on my thighs and held my head in my hands. Five minutes prior I didn't care who thought they had what. Sitting on that couch surrounded by people, I felt so alone and reasonably fearful of the little witch girl. She hadn't chased us through the crowd and up the stairs. As far as I knew, she hadn't even cared I was yelling in the middle of a crowd of lifestyle vampires exclaiming how fake I thought they were and putting their entire hierarchy into question. It didn't matter. Cyrus thought she was trouble and for some ridiculous reason, I actually trusted his opinion of others. Tatum was clueless, and as far as I could tell, so was her boyfriend. It could stay that way for all I cared.

Cyrus sat next to me. I could feel his glare burrowing into the back of my head. "Yeah?" I asked.

"This is what you plan to do for the evening?" He sounded a bit surprised that I'd basically told his boss to get fucked.

I nodded.

"You're not a bit concerned you just pissed of a fairly powerful voodoo priestess?"

Concerned? Yes. Terrified? Not really. Pissed the fuck off? Bingo.

"Should I be? Humph, can't be any worse than a set of kooky vampire boys out for blood." Pun intended.

"Those children were nothing in comparison." Cyrus definitely had a way of making things seem so much more dramatic than reality warranted.

"You act like you know this voodoo woman." For all I knew he did.

"In a way. Yes. I do. She has been practicing in this area for quite a long time and has built a… working relationship with the House of Porte." His hand trailed across my exposed back as he spoke.

"You mean to tell me you knew what I was getting into when I stepped foot into that ridiculous shop?" If he hadn't been touching me so nicely, I would have probably allowed an alcohol induced rant to sneak out.

"To be fair, your friend and I both asked you to leave. I know who she is, but there was no way for me to guess she would discover your past just as much as there was no way for you to guess. I know she is a long-standing practitioner and has a reputation for not being the most pleasant of the sort. If you want to know more, you must ask Marienne. What I can tell you is it is lucky for you that you are such an adamant nonbeliever." I felt the rumbling of his deep voice trail along the skin on my back.

"Oh yeah? And why is that?" I was beginning to feel the alcohol I'd consumed and it was rearing its snotty little head. Not to mention the evil intent I harbored for his master chief and my used-to-be-best friend.

"You have to believe something is true before your mind

begins to fear it. Until then, you're just an ignorant skeptic." I felt a shrug move along his body.

I wasn't looking at him and I was glad. I knew if I watched those idiotic words come out of that pretty mouth, I'd be more likely to bloody it up a bit. From a knock in the jaw, not by my willing donation.

"And what would happen if I did believe, do you think?" I held my mouth in a bitchy pursed lipped scowl not looking anywhere near Tatum and the mess she'd gotten herself into.

His hand continued its dance along the space between my shoulder blades. "You'd likely be fearful, and rightfully so. Madam Azelie is not someone you want as an enemy. Mystical powers aside, I've heard stories of her vengeful nature and I would not want to be on the receiving end of that vengeance."

"I don't understand what I've done to piss her off so badly. Badly enough I should be afraid of her."

Although, maybe I could hire her on to take care of the little ginger vamp problem I'm having.

"I'm not even certain you have. What I do know is, I saw the look in her eyes as she watched you from the stage. She was intentionally trying to intimidate you. I don't really know why, perhaps just because she doesn't like you. It really doesn't matter why, does it?"

"Sure as fuck does. If I pissed her off, then, whatever. I'll own it. But I didn't do anything. Okay, not enough to expect retaliation."

Not anything like the overtly guilty Malcolm McTavish who is a friend stealing, arrogant, shady-ass vampire boy.

"There is no guarantee you should be expecting anything from her. I am only warning you. Be careful. And by all means please don't piss anyone else off."

"Yeah, right." I scoffed drunkenly, and leaned back, rolling my head to the side to rest on the back of the circular couch.

I knew I'd gotten myself into quite a predicament. I just didn't know why, or how, or even to what extent. From what Cyrus was portraying, I should be shaking in my boots. But then he nearly contradicted himself and told me he wasn't even sure there was a threat in the first place. All I knew was the little voodoo woman was some kind of spooky. Regardless of whether or not I believed in her magical abilities, I'd learned from experience that people didn't have to actually have the power they thought they did. All they had to do was be fucking crazy enough to act on it to fuck shit up for everyone else. Hence, two vampire boys with a basement full of hooker blood.

"Another drink?" Cyrus asked and held an unknown beverage close to my face.

I felt like he'd roused me from a power nap. My eyes fluttered open and suddenly there was this delicious drink there in my face calling to me. I smiled crookedly and took the tiny glass. It seemed like all they were serving came in one and a half ounces of yummy. I was okay with that. Why waste calories on a mixer?

The alcohol tingled on its way down to my already booze-filled stomach. My eyes felt droopy and I was suddenly thankful for the sexy lace mask Cyrus had given me. Hide drunk behind lace, no one would be the wiser.

Allowing myself to relax, I turned on my ass and faced the truth. I was on the upper level of a vampire all-nighter, my best friend was drinking blood from her fire-crotch boyfriend, there very well could have been a vengeful high priestess after my ass, and I was getting drunker by the minute. Well, I'd be damned, if it wasn't a day in the life of Dylan Hart. The newfound fucking frightening life that it was. Why I'd allowed it all to unfold, I had no idea. Maybe life was boring before. I had to admit, I could get used to the danger of it all. It was pretty ironic how stupid humans pretending to be vampires caused more of a threat to me than the seedy Los Angeles public at large. Didn't make me carrying a gun to bed any less paranoid.

A nudge of an elbow brought me back to life. Apparently, I'd been resting my eyes. "Yes?" I said with more gumption than was necessary.

"Are you feeling alright?" asked a worried Cyrus.

Eyes still closed, I replied, "Fine. Just pondering my existence." I grinned at my own joke.

"Would you mind waking up and talking with me? I'm feeling a bit lonely stuck up here all by myself."

I opened my eyes and saw that the upper level had all but cleared out. Everyone, having filled themselves on liquor and blood, had retreated to the lower level to enjoy the open space of the dance floor. The band on stage had the crowd thrashing with their rhythmic beat.

"How long… where did…?" I really didn't have words. It seemed I'd lost my brain during my impromptu slumber.

"Not long. I let you sleep. I'd rather be up here if I had the choice." I could hear the smile in his voice. "Besides, you looked too cute to leave all alone. Someone may have come and taken you from me."

I let myself look in his direction. "Shut up," my voice came out scratchy. Something like a truck stop waitress. An uncontrollable smile spread across my numb lips as I saw his handsome face. He'd lost his jacket and leather mask at some point. "Thanks for not leaving me alone. Sorry I sacked, just got tired all of a sudden."

"You're a bit drunk." He laughed. "That is also cute."

"Jeez," I rolled my eyes as I blushed a cherry red and looked at my feet. "So, what now?" I asked with every intention in mind.

Tatum is having her fun. There is nothing in the rule books about Dylan Hart having to be bitter until the ends of time.

"Depends, would you like to join the other lemmings or would you like to stay up here with me?"

Both held promise, but the latter sounded much more satisfying. And safer. "We could stay up here a bit longer."

"Well, then, a drink?" He snickered and literally handed me a drink, holding one of his own in his large hand.

"Are you trying to get me drunk?" I asked as I took the drink. "Because you should know, I'd sleep with you anyway." It was my turn to laugh just before I took this last shot like a big tough guy.

"That is very good to know." His eyes sparkled in the flashing light from the lower level and reminded me of the night I'd first met him. The night I was so damned certain vampires were entirely on the up and up.

The two of us sat at a friendly distance from each other. Close enough to touch, but not so close I could deal out an old-fashion undetected. I couldn't look in those deep green eyes too long or I'd get lost in them, but I did allow one moment of pretty-eye gazing. His warm hand trailed over the clothed part of my thigh and I flinched. It'd been a while since I'd been actually hit-on and I'd kind of forgotten how it all went down.

"Hmm, sorry." I sucked at my lower lip. "Scared me a bit." I giggled like an idiot.

"I scared you? Why is that? I don't bite." He showed his white teeth in a large smile as he leaned closer to me. "Unless you ask."

"Ain't gon' happen *vampire* boy," a familiar and terrifying accent rolled toward us from the other end of the VIP section.

My heart decided to cease all function at the sound of her voice. The question was no longer *if* I'd pissed her off, it was how badly. And what in the fuck my punishment would be.

"You said we were safer here," I whispered as low as I could so he was still able to hear me but no one else.

"You in my town, *'cher*, you safe nowhere." The tiny woman stood a few dozen feet from our end of the loft. Still dressed in her stage costume, sans the snake, I could see her symbolic ink more clearly than I had before. They looked like something you'd see scrawled in chalk in a bad witchcraft movie. Only I was certain those were one hundred percent authentic. "You're not vampire," she stated, but seemed surprised by the epiphany.

She's just noticing this now?

I wasn't sure if that was a good thing or not. I also wasn't sure how she knew I wasn't part of the blood gang. Unless I was just that obvious. It really didn't matter how. If I knew how, I might have believed it. According to Cyrus, believing opened doorways to fear. I sure as fuck wasn't prepared to be scared.

In true Dylan fashion, my drunk ass said, "Nope. But who the fuck cares, eh? You're not all mighty." I wiggled my fingers in the air around my head. "Why don't you fuck off to fuckety off land and try your voodoo bullshit on someone who gives a crap because it's not working on me." I tried to stand but Cyrus stopped me. Probably for the best seeing as though I was likely too drunk to hold my own.

"Curse me as you like. I have curses, too." Her head dropped an inch and she stared at me under her lashes.

"Fuck your curses bitch!" I slurred and finally stood. Cyrus be damned. There was no way I was letting that little girl threaten me. Admittedly, I wasn't an idiot when it came to fighting fear. I hated being scared, hence all the anger. Anger was better. Anger fueled the fight.

I must have been drunker than I'd assumed because the girl, Madam Azelie, seemed to move so quickly toward me she was standing only feet from me before I could make a move. With her so close to me, I secretly prayed Cyrus would come to aid should my mouth talk me into something I couldn't get out of.

"Your body fight what your heart know is true." Her voice slithered from her pale pink lips and tickle along the hairs on the back of my neck. "You think your faith save you?" She laughed one hard heavy laugh, "Nothin' saves you." Her petite hand lifted, black rosary to dangling freely from her wrist. A God-fearing voodoo mama.

I opened my mouth to say something even more damaging than I had already spewed out, but the girl's outstretched hand swooped up and snatched me by my hair. "You will believe. Your heart belongs to me now," she whispered into my ear. Her hand wrenched into the thick mess of hair piled on top of my head. I teetered on my heels, but held my own. "She's yours Secondus. Have her while you can." Azelie released her grip in my hair, ripping a chunk out with it, and threw me back onto the couch.

I landed with a bounce and felt a spring dig into my bare knee. "Fuck." I grabbed my messy hair and held it to my aching head.

"Are you alright?" Cyrus asked as he used his hands to check my body for injuries.

My head lifted and my eyes darted around looking for my attacker. She'd gone. Just as quickly as she'd invaded our sanctuary, she'd disappeared. Bitch.

"Fine. What the fuck was that all about?" My heart pounded just about out of my chest and I thought I might vomit. If I wasn't scared before, I was now. Not because I believed she'd curse me or that she had some kind of magical power, but because I learned the hard way she was crazy enough to turn make-believe into reality. You didn't snatch a bitch up by the hair unless you were ready to fight. It just wasn't done.

"It seems our uncertainties have been confirmed. She's pissed." He laughed, but I knew he was trying to make light of the situation. When people tried to make things seem better than they were, it usually meant it was pretty damn bad.

"Well, obviously." I flopped backward and leaned into the cushioned back of the couch. "I am far too drunk for this shit." I grabbed my forehead with one hand and rubbed my head with the other.

"Maybe it's time to leave. Would you like to leave with me?" he asked like I'd say no.

I whirled a finger in the air above my head. "Let's blow this blood bank." I stood too fast and stumbled.

"Should I carry you?" Cyrus asked as he caught my fall.

"Yeah, you and what army?" I laughed and regained my balance.

He held my arm to steady me as we descended the stairs together. Normally, I'd have protested, but I was drunk and a bit randy. I was not about to ask him to stop touching even on principle. I nervously surveyed our surroundings as we made our way through the crowd. All we needed to do was get out those two doors and we were clear. Then we had to make the fifteen-minute walk back to the car in the darkened New Orleans streets. Drunk. And on the radar of the voodoo queen of New Orleans.

Fuck.

We stopped in the center of the dance floor where Tatum and

Malcolm were devouring each other. "We're leaving. I'll need the car." We'd interrupted them. Fuck 'em. "Sir, it's urgent." Cyrus pressed.

"Fine, fine. Take the girl home." Malcolm pulled his lower lip under his teeth with a grin. "Be gentle with her, Cyrus. She's a delicate one." He laughed and scooped Tatum up into his bare arms and walked away with her. I ignored his warning to Cyrus and took the delicate part as a compliment.

"Have fun!" Tatum called from the shoulder of her beau and waved at me.

I wanted to hate her, but it was never going to happen. I would sooner get over my own bullshit and give in than her succumb to my pleading. Besides, there were more pressing matters at hand than whether or not my friend wanted to hang out.

Cyrus groaned and dragged me deeper into the thick of vampy kids. Capes and wings flipped around in a never-ending dance around us. If filmed in slow motion, our escape would have made for a phenomenal music video. The two of us slid effortlessly through the hordes of lace, coat tails, top hats, and fangs. Cyrus's beautiful body led the way in the rescue of his damsel in distress. Damsel I was not. Ever. Would I have argued at that moment? Fuck no. I wasn't an idiot. Usually.

We made it to the double doors and Cyrus shoved them open with his muscled shoulder. More vamp kids stood out front waiting to be allowed in. We pushed through them and to a waiting car at the curb. I stopped in my tracks and refused to enter the unknown car.

Where the fuck did this car come from? What is this Knight Rider?

"Come on, I'm not kidnapping you. We'll need a ride to our car." His words weren't overly reassuring, but I didn't really have a choice.

I slid in the back, flashing my ass to the world, and Cyrus

was right behind me.

"Waterfront lot," he said to the driver.

"Where did this car come from? Some kind of vampire telepathy called for a car?" It sounded ridiculous as it came out of my mouth.

"No," he said like I was an idiot. "It's a sober car. Mostly here for the Primus and Secondus, we all need to get home somehow." It was as if I should have been aware of this my entire life the way he talked about it.

Where I came from you sucked it up and drove that shit one-eyed. Their way was admittedly better.

"So, that woman, she's not going to pop up at random and take a pound of flesh, is she? I'm just asking to be prepared next time." Right.

"She will not be allowed near you if I can prevent it. I can guarantee she will not follow you to our house and your weekend should be more pleasurable than it has been so far as long as you stay with me and out of trouble."

As long as I didn't have to lay my eyes on Tatum and the ridiculousness of her life, I should've been able to focus on research. Oh, and getting laid.

"Well, here's hoping." I smiled and tried to wink.

Scary bitches be damned, Dylan Hart did not turn down opportunities to nail underwear models; Secondus of the House of Cal… whatever. Not that I'd ever been in that particular situation before, but why the fuck would I start turning that shit down on a whim?

Vampire boys, voodoo queens, and drunk bitches. What the hell else would you expect from a weekend in New Orleans?

This shit cannot be normal.

TEN

I SAT SHOTGUN IN OUR FANCY RENTAL CAR, DRUNK, AND staring at the gorgeous man at the wheel. The long sexless stretch of months had been an anomaly for me. Fat or not I got play. This particular bout of celibacy had been unintended and likely had a lot to do with my emotional crustiness post vigilantism.

Smiling lazily, I giggled like stupid girl. "You're pretty." I still had that stupid mask on my face and it wasn't helping anything.

He smiled with his entire face and said, "As are you."

"Liar, liar, pants on fire." I knew I sounded ridiculous, but I couldn't stop myself. I was usually good at hiding a slur, but there was no hiding whatever the hell I was trying to do or the supremely drunk motivation behind it.

"Believe me or not, that is entirely up to you. And, knowing you, you never will." His eyes were trained on the street ahead of us.

We stopped at a red light, which had no reason to be red, and waited our time. I thought, or tried to think, about what he'd said. About me never believing him. To a point, he was absolutely right. He'd hidden truths from me that nearly got me killed. How did you trust someone after something like that? Not to mention, why in the fuck would a guy like Cyrus Atossa even look twice at a dumpy ass like me? It didn't happen, ever. My gut told me he had a hidden agenda. My sexual frustration told me I'd better get while the getting was good. And dammit it was good.

I pulled the lace mask from my face and sat quietly, thinking of things better left to the imagination. The car remained silent the last five minutes before we reached our destination. It wasn't for lack of things to say. I had plenty to say. To ask. I just figured it'd be better to wait until the time was right. When I wasn't totally sloshed. And trying to get laid.

I'd hardly waited for him to shift into park when, with all the grace I could muster, I slung my stocking clad leg over his lap. In one fluid motion, I flipped my big ass over the center console to sit on his lap. I took a moment to congratulate myself for not totally fucking up potentially the slickest move I'd ever pulled and re-centered my focus on the handsome face inches from mine.

His green eyes went wind before a bright smile pushed them into half-moons. "Dylan Hart, where have you been hiding this vixen?" His minty breath warmed my cheeks.

I was suddenly self-conscious about my own swamp mouth. I knew, just knew, it couldn't smell fresh. In fact, the likelihood my breath smelled like something that crawled out of a dumpster was high.

"You are quite lovely," Cyrus said with utmost certainty.

"As are you," I tried to talk without letting air escape my mouth; it never worked.

It unexpectedly dawned on me that I was sitting spread eagle, in an amazing car, perched atop an underwear model who also happened to be the Secondus for the House of vampire crap, and I was one-hundred percent awake. Granted also horribly inebriated, but that was beside the point.

This cannot be my life.

Sitting the way I was, acting as slutty as I could pull off rationally, it was inevitable. The big *it*. I got uncomfortable when someone looked at me with some sort of expectation, I always fucked up at *that* moment. I felt Cyrus staring a hole in the side of my head as I let my gaze linger out the driver side window. My body leaned toward his, nearly pressed chest to chest, but I couldn't bring myself to keep my eyes locked on his. I didn't know if it was because of their perfection or because of my imperfections, but meeting his eyes made me feel helpless. Like I was his little lap dog panting and dancing at his feet begging for a treat. A pet. A scratch behind the ears. Anything would do. It was as if I was staring into the one thing I couldn't fight off. Couldn't say no to. I'd tried in the past and finally gave up on looking at his face all together. Well, directly anyway. In reality, sitting as I was, if I didn't look at him, nothing would ever happen.

His hand trailed up the center of my back and down again leaving a heat memory on my skin. I pulled a long, deep breath in through my nose to calm my nerves and with it dragged in his scent. He always smelled so clean. So masculine. I felt his breath on my neck and decided to make my move.

I turned my head to face his before I lost the nerve. I wanted him, sure. But I wasn't generally the type of girl to throw herself at someone. Unless very drunk, which I was, so it made no difference. My head turned and met his only an inch away. My world spun as I did and I felt, for the first time, truly and utterly drunk. I swallowed hard and tried to push the inebriation down. My eyes focused on his lips, so close to mine I was nearly cross-eyed looking at them. A slight grin slid over that perfect pouty mouth. He shifted his weight under me and tightened his arms to pull me closer to him.

I closed my eyes and waited. Beginning to feel too drunk to pursue my conquest without utter failure, I allowed him to take over. His nose nuzzled against mine and I smiled. It was cute. Not what I was looking for. He slid his face to the side of mine and kissed along my cheek so softly I could hardly tell they were kisses. He trailed his lips across my skin and lingered an inch from my lips. Soft lips touched the corner of my mouth and stayed there. Cyrus shifted his body again, but this time, with my eyes closed, it sent a wave of drunken dizziness through my head.

I fought the spins and tried to stay with him. His hands reached up and pulled the pins from my wild hair. All my wavy locks came falling to my shoulders. His mouth, an inch from mine, lingered in limbo, not touching me, but close enough it could happen in an instant. Cyrus didn't even bother running his hands through my mess of hair. I was glad. He touched it, ran his hand over it, and I think he even gave it a sniff. I'd never really been with anyone who took their time as Cyrus did. We hadn't even kissed each other full on the mouth and I felt I'd been more intimate with him than anyone in my life. Mike included.

Heavy hands held my hair in a snug, slightly domineering grip. I kind of liked it. Cyrus slid his lips across my cheek again, but was not stopping. My heart raced in anticipation. My stomach flipped and fluttered with it. His lips grazed mine and I realized it wasn't anticipation.

He pressed his mouth to my lips and I pushed him away instantly. I wasn't fast enough. Bile filled vomit came pouring from my once sensual lips and splattered his handsomely tailored shirt .

I clamped a hand on my mouth and fumbled for the door handle. I found it in record time and tumbled from the car onto the spongy grass that lined the sidewalk in front of the manor where we were staying. My ass stuck up in the air while I crawled on my knees to a safer place to release the remaining contents of my stomach. As I wretched in the gutter in front of a vampire infested southern mansion, I worried about the effect this particular event would have on my psyche. And more importantly at that very moment, what kind of affect it would have on the remainder of the weekend.

I heard the car door close and cringed. I was finished puking my guts out, but I hated to look up and see what I'd made of the lovely man I'd so nearly gotten my grubby little hands on.

"I'm so sorry," I sputtered out still lying in the wet grass.

There was no response. I wiped my face with the back of my hand and wiped that hand on the grass. Checking the front of my dress for remnants of vomit, I was grateful Cyrus had been holding my hair for me when it all came out. I was clear of leftovers and didn't want to see what I'd left all over Cyrus' black suit.

I rolled over onto my ass and looked up. Cyrus stood nearly over the top of me. Shirtless. My jaw dropped and I was instantly thankful I'd puked. Although, if I hadn't, Lord knew where I'd have been at that moment. If you were gonna vomit on your date, at least revel in the fact he must be without his clothing. I thanked God for small miracles.

I knew I looked a hot mess and smelled like hot garbage. Sloppily, I groped the shoes off my feet. I'd never have stood up on my own wearing those bad boys. On wobbly legs, I lifted my heavy frame disagreeably from the wet grass. I felt like a complete and total fucktard.

Cyrus laughed and ran his hand through his hair. A motion I would expect from the likes of Michael Petersen not Cyrus Atossa. So… normal. He was laughing at me. I stood, as best I could, and slammed both fists on my hips. My face scrunched and I glared at him. So fucking drunk I couldn't handle myself.

Without a further word, Cyrus swooped my fat ass up in his arms and carried me. He didn't just pick me up. He picked me up, draped over his arms like a bride, and carried me to the front door. I felt so fucking fat. I knew he was going to drop me. Or get too tired and make me walk. I waited for further embarrassment. It never came.

I relaxed when we came to the door and nearly fell asleep after the first set of stairs. By the time he carried me to my room, I was so worried about him and flabbergasted he was able to lift me up let alone carry me all that way. Shit, I had a hard enough time carrying my own body up those stairs.

His hot skin pressed against my arm. He never said a word. I was afraid to open my mouth for fear the stench of bile would waft out. His scent was still lovely and masked anything I had left on me. My face was snuggled, drunk and comfortable in his chest when he lowered me onto my bed. I was sad to have to leave his arms. I was even more mortified I'd fucking puked on him.

"I'm so sorry," I slurred. I tried to look at him, but my eyes wouldn't focus and twisted my view.

"Just sleep," he said in a tone that told me absolutely nothing about what he was thinking.

I felt his weight leave the edge of the bed and my hand

automatically reached for him. I caught his arm and he stopped. A tiny noise came from my throat and he laughed. His weight returned. I was relieved he didn't despise me, but worried he'd stuck around purely for revenge. His warmth helped me forget it all.

He relaxed next to me. I felt his hand slide over my hair before his fingers began twisting bits of it between them. The world spun from my spot on my borrowed bed and I rolled with it. There was nothing left in my stomach to throw up so I had no worries of further pea soup moments. If I were at home, I'd have been in the shower, guzzling down water, and popping aspirin like it was candy. But I was stuck in a darkened and totally foreign environment. Strangely enough, the only person I had to rely on was Cyrus Atossa. The person who drove me nuts from the moment I'd met him had quickly become my only ally. Thanks to Tatum and the fire crotch, it seemed like I might have been Cyrus's only ally too.

Blackness was taking over and my breathing was falling in line with my heart beat. Numb limbs laid haphazardly on the overstuffed bed and conveniently on the man who decided to lie next to me. It was the first time I'd laid, just laid down with a man since Mike, and if I hadn't been fucked up beyond belief, it probably would have been awkward. Thankfully, I was a lush.

Before sleep took over, I hoped to God I'd wake up and Cyrus would still be there and that he'd have mysteriously forgotten the whole thing. But I knew it was more likely I'd wake up and have forgotten the whole thing. I'd set out to get laid, finally, and I fucked it all up by barfing on my suitor. In pure Dylan Hart fashion.

Living, breathing, puking, conundrum.

ELEVEN

WE LAY SLEEPING IN A BED OF WHITE. PLUSH, OVERSTUFFED pillows billowed around our heads. In matching white Long Johns, I snuggled spooning with a child about half my size. Her curly brunette locks mimicked mine and waved around her head like sea foam. Our bare feet overlapped one another and my arm draped over her side. We both slept soundly. I saw the two of us from a bird's eye view as if watching from outside my own body. The little girl I lay with seemed so similar to me. I wondered if I was seeing my own child. A futuristic premonition of my child and I asleep in our bed.

Bright white light filtered through unseen windows, illuminating the stark snowy bedding. The contrast between our dark hair and the white of the linen was shocking and ethereal. Neither of us moved. Not even a sleepy little twitch. Like two mannequins snuggled on a bed, alone in a room of white. Suddenly and with no obvious discretion, syrupy red liquid fell from above my view. I watched as sheets of it dropped in slow motion down toward the sleeping child and my own body. A spark in my core told me to stop the carnage. Prevent this scene from presenting itself to the girl sleeping so peacefully. But it proved pointless to try. I was only a bystander, innocent I was not, but bystander nonetheless. I had no hands, no voice, no vessel with which to halt the impending gore.

The moment I realized there was nothing that could be done, the red ooze splashed onto its target. The beautiful little girl lay in her lush white bed covered from head to toe in thick crimson blood. Her clean white pajamas soaked to her skin with it. My clothing was the same. Our hair stuck in wet ribbons to the pillows we laid on, and our intertwined bare feet dripped blood from their toes. In all the mess, neither body moved. No one awoke in screaming hysterics. Through the spreading blood, I watched as a tiny smirk spread across the face of the child. In horror, I looked to my own face hidden poorly behind a mask of blood and saw an identical grin. The child and I slept in a bed of blood and I think we liked it.

I sat up in my borrowed four-poster bed and held my head in my hands. I tried hard not to cry, but failed miserably. My thoughts flashed on the face of the little girl in that lovely bed. The little girl who looked so much like me. So innocent lying in a bed of white. So cynical covered in blood boasting a maniacal grin. I thought, for the first time in a long time, about my dad. I was a little girl once. A little girl with long curly brown hair. A little girl who looked so much like her handsome daddy. A little girl spattered with the blood and brain matter from the back of her daddy's head after someone shot him through the windshield of his car.

Years of therapy had taught me to move past that night, to forget the images that were ingrained in my little head, and to allow those thoughts to flow through now and then and not become a complete psycho. Therapy worked. Having a mother who loved me unconditionally helped. Having a friend like Tatum who was there to back me up at any given moment helped. Having my darling Mike love me for all that I was and all that I wasn't helped. After a while, I didn't need all that support. Shit, I didn't want it.

They were always so fucking worried about fragile little Dylan. I'd made myself forget that night, made myself move on from it. Remembering my dad for who he was not how he died. It worked. Even through all the blood that night in Mission Junction, it didn't affect me. Didn't affect me, so much so, I seemed a bit sociopathic. Maybe I was.

"God, maybe I'm just a fucking nutcase," I whispered to myself in my darkened room and felt a little ridiculous.

After all those years of forcing myself to be unaffected, one bloody little dream brought it all out. Well, not all, but a little bit of crazy leaked out. I sniffed the snot back up into my nose, and wiped my wet cheeks. A familiar cynical smirk moved along my lips and I spoke into the darkness one more time.

"Dad, I miss you. If anytime you can come to visit, please make it now. I need you." I'd said that line more than once in the twenty years since that horrific night and not once had he answered. Not that I could hear or see anyway.

It wasn't often I allowed myself to think of him or the night he died. It was better that way, I thought. But sitting alone in the pitch dark in the center of the spookiest place in the south, it seemed fairly appropriate to speak to the dead.

I wondered if the little witch girl, Azelie, was psychic enough to talk to my dad. The moment the thought entered my head, I flushed it away. It was crazy to even think it. First of all, she was a fucking lunatic. Secondly, I sort of trusted Cyrus. He said to stay away, so I figured I'd listen to someone else for once and maybe save my own ass. Aside from running into the crazy bitch at social events, of course.

My head spun for a moment and I remembered how drunk I'd been hours before. Or days. Or months. Fuck, it was impossible to live in real time with no window. It made for constant darkness. An endless night moving from one darkened space to another.

The light from the screen of my charging phone was the only thing allowing me to make out the shapes in the room. My door was closed and I slept alone. A quick check told me I was dressed in my pajamas and even wore a pair of socks I didn't remember putting on. I'd been awake for quite a few minutes worrying over the past before I noticed the present. What the fuck did that say about me?

On socked feet, I moved from the comfort of my bed to the dresser that held my phone. The only lifeline I had to the outside world. It seemed I was losing Tatum with every passing minute and I hated Malcolm McTavish so uncontrollably it was a wonder he didn't make it into my staked bank.

Haha. Staked bank. I'm so fucking clever.

The only other person I felt I could at least trust not to throw me to the wolves was Cyrus. And even that was questionable. I was growing thankful he'd been such a gentleman. There was no way I would have made it up those stairs on my own and judging by the fact I was wearing socks, it was likely he helped me change my clothes.

A mortified thought passed through my head when I realized he'd removed my clothing. He'd seen me naked. In a panic, I grabbed my boobs to check for a bra. A relieved breath escaped my lips when I felt the familiar padding of my strapless bra. He hadn't taken it all off. Only what was necessary before putting on my pants and a t-shirt.

Relieved, I smiled. Bloody little girls and dead daddies abound and my biggest concern was whether or not a hot guy saw my tits. What the fuck was wrong with me? Perhaps a few more therapy sessions were in order. A lot more.

Requiring the presence of someone living, I left my room of dark solitude and sought out a familiar face. I knew the room across the hall was the temporary home of one of my favorite little vampy boys, but I wasn't exactly comfortable with just knocking at his door. He had stripped me naked, so the embarrassment to follow when I did see him was going to be great for certain. I figured I might as well put that off as long as I could. Besides, there was another party to attend, giving me an entirely new opportunity to do something completely ridiculous. What was a weekend getaway without utter embarrassment?

The hall was dark and Cyrus's door was closed. No light spilled from under his door so I assumed he was still sleeping. I glanced at my phone to check the time. The bright screen told me it was seven-fourteen. I'd only been asleep a few hours as far as I could tell. I doubted anyone else would be awake at that hour. It was a surprise that I was.

My socked feet made no noise as they moved along the carpeted floor on the third level. A few other doors lined the dark hallway, but all were closed. I realized I had no clue which room was Tatum's. Not as though I'd have gone barreling into a room she shared with that ginger vampire boy anyway. Just the principle of the thing. What if there were an emergency? I supposed that was why I was shoved with Mr. Atossa for the weekend. I questioned if it was Tatum or Cyrus who asked that I be invited on the bloody getaway. It would have made a lot of sense. And yet, none and all. Why in the holy hell would the guy I put a bullet through have wanted to invite me on vacation with him and his vampy friends? It was yet another question added to my ever-growing list of shit that didn't make sense.

Giving up on finding the living on the third floor, I made my way down the modest stairway to the much more extravagant second level. There was no noise coming from anywhere in the general vicinity. No moving bodies. No silly little bloodletting ceremonies clogging up the second floor landing, just a beautiful southern mansion filled with things older than me by a hundred years. And no, not the inhabitants. No matter how much they wanted it to be true, those little vampire kids did not live forever unless staked. Human, just like me and you. Only, they liked to drink a little blood now and then. No big deal. Right.

The wide, sweeping stairs that led to the main floor lay just ahead. The house was so dark and quiet you'd think it was the middle of the night instead of first thing in the morning. I reached the stairs and felt a twinge of fear in my stomach. The kind that made you turn to see if someone's following you. There was no one around, but that didn't make me any less creeped out. There was something about wandering through an old southern mansion in near blackness that was pretty fucking scary. Maybe it was just me being a chicken.

Fear driving me to move faster, my little feet pounded each step in a desperate effort to reach the main floor and a large set of windows by the front doors. Reaching the ground level at the speed of fat ass, my socked feet nearly slid out of control on the slick hardwood floor. I caught myself on the winding railing. My heavy breathing grew more rapid every moment I didn't see light, every moment I was stuck in the grand open space full of so many spooky opportunities.

Practically sliding, I reached one of the floor length curtains and flung each back and away from the window beneath it. My eyes grew wide and my breath caught at the sight before me. Instead of a glorious light filled window, I was met with dark wooden shutters closed from the outside. No light peaked through the trap of darkness.

"Fuck me," I said in a tone so near a breath it couldn't even be called a whisper.

In a flash, I moved to the tall double doors. My hands tugged and twisted at the old brass knobs, desperately trying to pry them open. Each was locked. I used my phone to illuminate the mechanism. No deadbolt on the old-fashioned doors. Each was locked with a key from the inside. Panic was setting in. It seemed to me I was locked in a monstrous Victorian tomb with a gaggle of blood drinking idiots. Not to mention the all-around creep factor of the dark scary house.

The drapes that led to the parlor were open and seemed inviting to the desperate. Using my phone to light the way, I made it to the smaller more furnished room. In the dark and not filled with plastic fanged people lying about, it seemed lonely somehow. I shined the light from my phone into every corner and onto every wall. There was not a window to be found.

In the dark, my mind made up all sorts of scary things I'd run into. One of which was the big bad voodoo bitch. I imagined her bright blue eyes peering out at me from a darkened corner.

Giving up on the search, I devised a plan. I'd run as quickly as I could back to my room and wake Cyrus. Embarrassment be damned. Unadulterated fear was beginning to seep in and take over. Fear usually took precedence on the grand scheme of emotions. Anger coming in at a close second.

A few quick breaths in and out for courage, and I was off like a rocket. Slippery socks slid across the well-polished flooring. I made it to the stairs in record time, but slid out of control trying to stop at the first step. Again, I grabbed the thick wooden spire that protruded from the winding railing. Careening out of control, my body followed its forward momentum. I spun around on the axis my clenched hand had created, and slammed into the railing on the outside of the staircase.

A little door under the stairs slowly opened. When I hit the railing, I'd heard a pop and assumed it was something detrimental in my body breaking. It became apparent I'd likely jarred the little door from its closure. The miniature wooden door opened without a sound and stood awaiting a nosey little snoop to see what was beyond it. One of the only things that could surpass fear was curiosity. I was one curious bitch. It may have killed the cat, but satisfaction brought it back. And damn if I wasn't unsatisfied.

I stood for a moment and allowed my heart to slow its pace. Forcing my rationale to take over and snuff the unwarranted fear, I waited also for one of the many inhabitants to come investigate all the noise. No one came. I listened for any microscopic noise to warn me of the presence of someone. Nothing. I used this silence as a sign I was meant to investigate what lay behind that tiny door. In true sleuth fashion, I tiptoed to the short opening. A secret part of me wished I had theme music playing lightly in the background. Maybe a magnifying glass in hand for good measure.

I stuck the face of my lit phone through the opening first. A set of narrow stone steps led down to a dimly lit basement. At the end of the steps, from a source unseen, a soft golden glow made its way up the narrow passage illuminating the stairs. It was nice to see some form of light. Even if it was hidden at the bottom of a set of tiny stairs. I listened again. Not a sound. I was beginning to feel as though I had earplugs in my ears. There was always something making noise. A clock ticking, a cricket chirping, a fucking tree blowing in the breeze outside. Something. But I heard nothing.

Before I could make the conscious choice, my feet carried me down the steps into the unknown below. The light grew brighter the nearer I reached the end of the steps. Relief began to wash over me as I bathed in the golden light.

At the bottom of the stairs, the room opened to either side leaving a narrow space between the foot of the steps and a wall just in front of me. I stood on the last step and leaned me body forward to look in either direction. Small walls on both sides prevented my snooping.

I took a deep breath and picked a side. Left.

Around the stone partition, curiosity met its match. The light I'd seen from the top of the stairwell emanated from a dozen brass gaslight sconces. After a quick count, I knew there were exactly seven ornate coffins lined up perfectly in the center of the area. One white, one black, one a beautiful cherry wood. It looked like a funeral home show room. I wondered if they were lined in satin for a second before panic set in.

I knew I'd been sleeping in a house with people who liked to drink a little blood, have a little fun, and pretty much get down tonight, but I didn't know it was this far down. Like coffins in the fucking basement down. It was one thing to dress up and play make-believe, it was a whole other thing to sleep in a goddamned coffin.

My chest rose and fell with each heavy breath I gulped. I wondered if Malcolm was in one of those. If Tatum knew it. Before my feet turned and tore ass out of the room of death, I wondered if Cyrus was down there somewhere. I turned with such adrenaline my eyes weren't even working yet. I slammed directly into a hard object and it wasn't a stone wall.

A scream escaped my lungs and in a fit I began slamming fists into the chest of the object I'd run into. My eyes were closed tight, and my fists hit as hard as I could, but nothing was coming of it. No sound from the thing I'd been hitting. Only my own screams. I shoved my body into the person in my way trying to escape the basement. It didn't move. It didn't react. Just a blockade of flesh in my way. It wouldn't have mattered anyhow. The front door was fucking Fort Knox. I was stuck in the hell I'd walked right into. I forced my eyes to open and saw my captor.

Cyrus stood before me in all of his beautiful splendor . My heart stopped. He smiled a sardonic grin and a set of menacing fangs made their way to the forefront.

"No. No." I shook my head side to side in an effort to shake away the unbelievable.

My feet took a few shaky steps back and away from my once confidant. His strong arms reached for me. Thick hands enveloped my upper arms and squeezed in a show of dominance. My eyes locked on his deep stare. I remembered the sensation I'd felt the first time I'd gotten lost in those supernatural eyes. I heard a whimper and realized it was coming from my throat.

I was terrified, but intensely engrossed in the eyes of Cyrus Atossa, Secondus, House of Cailleadh. Vampire aficionado. Sexiest man who'd ever laid his hands on me. Death incarnate.

Pointed fangs shone horrifically in the light of a dozen gas lamps as the beautiful vampire boy opened his mouth and threatened a strike. Even with his face in a deathly snarl, he was still the prettiest boy I'd ever had the pleasure of falling victim to. Knowing there was no escape, I accepted my fate. It was quite unlike me to accept anything at face value, but I did. Honestly, a part of me hoped it was true. Hoped they were all honest to goodness vampires. Hoped instead of draining my body of its life force, Cyrus would decide to take me over to the undead side. To live forever young and beautiful. Young anyway.

He lowered his head to meet the crook of my neck. I didn't protest. I didn't shove him away. Slap his face. Knee him in the nuts. Nothing. I just let him fucking do it. The tips of pointed fangs poked the tender skin at my neck and I braced myself for the pain to come. My heart fluttered in anticipation. I was scared to death of the pain, but in a way, excited about the possibilities. I tiny piece of my heart knew he wouldn't kill me. Believed deep down he had a soul and would never take mine from me. At least not without replacing it with immortal life. I closed my eyes and tried to embrace the danger. Allow myself to feel wanted, if only for my delicious blood. And somewhere inside, wanted it right back.

The pressure from the tips of his fangs became too great and the skin of my neck finally gave way with a pop. Lips touched the soft area of my neck and he drew in his first taste of my blood. It took my breath from my lungs to feel my blood escape my body and enter his warm mouth. His hands squeezed my arms with intensity, heat emanated from the tips of his fingers, like a fire under my skin. He pulled me in closer to him. His chest rose and fell with excited breaths. Another whimper rolled deep in my chest, and his strong arms rocked my body with a jolt. It was an odd motion and didn't correlate with the situation. Again, his arms jolted and shook my body with them. I squealed from high in my throat and squeezed my eyes tighter in pain. His jerking rocked my body with a deep ache. Another jolt of his arms. And another. Another. Until he was shaking me back and forth. His teeth still sunk deep in my neck. I screamed with every jar of my body as each movement tore at the tender flesh of my neck.

Screams came with tears and my fists again came up and began punching at his shoulders and arms. I wanted him to stop. I didn't want death anymore. The pain was so great, I thought I'd pass out, but I forced myself to fight him off. To live through the horrific encounter and kill the bastard the second I got the chance. I hit as hard as I could and felt his grip tighten as he shook me harder.

"Dylan? Dylan?" I heard him say as if we communicated through a can and string. It sounded so far away.

His mouth was pressed to the flesh of my throat. Why is he calling my name? I thought, wildly trying to make sense of the situation. Frantically, I flung my fists in his direction hoping one would hit home.

"Dammit, Dylan." A slap hit me across my face and I opened my eyes.

My clenched fist swung with all my might. The sound of meat slapping meat, I'd hit my target. Blood spurted from the mouth of Cyrus Atossa, Secondus, House of Cailleadh, bastard.

I clamped a hand over my mouth in shock. My wide eyes

took in their surroundings with utter remorse.

Where the hell did all those coffins go?

TWELVE

CYRUS SAT ON THE EDGE OF MY BED HOLDING HIS JAW. BLOOD drizzled down his chin from the split in his lip I'd given him. Lying in my bed, in my borrowed room, in the dress I'd partied in all night, I watched Cyrus Atossa, Secondus, House of Cailleadh, bleeding from his perfect face.

Fuck.

"Oh, my God. Oh, my God. Are you okay?" I asked frantically.

"Are *you* okay? You were screaming so loudly I could hear you from my room." He rubbed his jaw in small circles.

"I guess… I guess I was dreaming." I furrowed my brow and I shook my head in disbelief. A dream within a dream? Where the fuck was Leo D. to save the day?

"I guess," he said sarcastically, still theatrically rubbing his jaw to prove his point.

"I said I was sorry." After the dream I'd just come out of, he was lucky I was still sitting there watching him bleed. My hand lifted on its own and rubbed along my neckline. Everything was still intact.

"What were you dreaming about that had you so frightened?" He looked at me with such sorrowful eyes I wondered if he knew it was about him.

"Something scary apparently," I said simply.

He smiled through the damage to his perfect mouth, "Thanks for the wakeup call." A thick red slit peered at me from his bottom lip and I winced. Only a little.

"What time is it?" I asked. Feeling a bit embarrassed as the events from the night before flooded into my memory. I knew I'd been pretty damned drunk. At least, unlike my dream, I was still wearing my clothes. No one stripped me naked.

Damn.

"Just after six." I stared at him. No light in my room wasn't only a dream, it was a piece of reality seeping in. "P.M."

I continued to stare at him astonished, "You've got to be kidding me. How long was I sleeping?"

He chuckled lightly and I swore I saw a blush flush into his cheeks. "A while. It was after five in the morning last I glanced at you. You were sleeping soundly then." The look on his face told me he was trying very hard not to laugh. I thought quickly about what had happened, if there had been anything I should've been aware of before I finished our conversation. I couldn't remember much past the after party. All I knew was he'd slept in the bed next to me for the better part of my comatose state.

No coffins. No horrific gnawing at the neck region. And likely lots of snoring and drooling. Fuck.

"All fucking day? Shit." I laughed a little. "I dreamt I woke up and it was so dark I didn't know what time it was. It was disorienting. Still is." I smiled and looked down at my hands. It was hard enough looking at him on a good day. Let alone on the day I dreamt he was trying to kill me, then subsequently, cold cocking him in the face.

"Yes. The light is… frowned upon in this house. A bit of extremists at the House of Porte. Marienne, the Primus, prefers her home sun-free." He smiled and looked more normal than he had ever.

"Really?" I replayed my dream in my head. No sun. All the windows were shut up downstairs and the front door was locked tight. So as to not allow in any undue light. "Pretty extreme, huh?" I nodded soaking it in. Extreme enough to keep a stock pile of coffins in the basement perhaps?

"Yes. More so than Malcolm I'd say. More traditional. Malcolm sees our… situation as more of an opportunity for profit than revering in the culture."

"How many other Houses feel the same way?" I asked trying to sound interested but not chomping at the bloody bit. Which I was, but he didn't need to know that.

"As Malcolm?"

I nodded.

"Not many. Malcolm is a special breed." He laughed at his own joke and I smiled to be nice. It really wasn't funny. "Most Houses are traditional, with traditional beliefs. A few don't even take part in these annual events because they feel it's not smart to include the public in our culture."

"Really? How many houses are there?"

"Quite a many . You can bet nearly every state has one, New York has three," he said, as if it was a big deal. "With the exception of Utah, you should be able to find a Primus residing in every state."

"Why not Utah?"

"Could you imagine a place like Macabre Saturnine popping up in Utah?" he laughed and so did I. That was actually a humorous notion.

"So, each house has a Primus and a Secondus. Why?"

"It's always been." His hand moved to his lip and wiped away the last of the blood from his mouth. The red slit remained blood free for the time being.

"Since… the seventies?" I laughed too loudly. "I mean, how long have there really been Sanguinarians? Since Anne Rice?" I was still chuckling when he looked at me and stole my breath. "I'm sorry. It just all seems a little over-the-top. It's all make-believe. Obviously, someone went to a lot of trouble coming up with all of this. Houses, Primus, Secondus, rules of house, ceremonies, all of it, just seems a bit much."

"Perhaps to you, a mundane." He actually turned his nose up at me just a bit.

"What did you call me? Look, Cyrus, I've noticed the last few days you're kinda shit on around here. Well, mostly by Malcolm. I just don't understand why you deal with it. It's like sticking around a D&D game when someone is kicking you in the nuts all night." Pointless and a bit silly if you asked me.

Regardless of nightmares of coffin-filled rooms and yearnings to be bit by the lovely Cyrus Atossa, I knew it was all pretend. A fun little game made up by those who wanted to truly be immortal. Far be it for me to stop them, let your freak flag fly, but in the end if you couldn't admit it was fake didn't that make you a little nutty?

Maybe just as nutty as the girl who dreams of dead daddies and vampires?

"It's best you don't allow anyone in this house hear you refer to them and their life as a game of D&D." His tone was of the serious variety, as was his expression.

"But you have to understand where I'm coming from here, right? You have to know this isn't real."

Unless of course it is in which case we have an entirely new can of graveyard worms on our hands.

"I'm not the one in question here. It's the House of Porte that concerns you?" he said, as if he already knew, with utmost certainty, I was prying into the lives of the inhabitants of the home I was sleeping in. As much as he knew, somehow, in the back of my head , I was afraid of the house. Of New Orleans, and the things I'd learned. The things I would learn.

"Yes. I guess in a way you're right. Tell me more about the Houses. How does this work? Who is the founder of all this nonsen… er… rich culture?" I raise my brows and changed my tone to a lighter more sarcastic attitude.

"The founder of the House of Cailleadh was a man named Nicolas Sandorus."

"Sandorus? Like Sandora?" Malcolm's magazine and a pretty vampire girl I'd met in Fresno.

He chuckled a bit. "Yes, you remember. I told you once before, Sandora is a popular nightside name for our ladies. Nicolas, Nico, Sandorus was the first Primus of the House of Sandora, now called the House of Cailleadh. I was his Secondus before Malcolm came. House of Sandora was not located in southern California, but still was the representing House for the state of California. Sandorus represented the Western Cabal from his seat as Primus. As Marienne represents the Southern Cabal. As Malcolm does now in the West."

Wonder if Huell Howser has an episode on this rich history of California? California's Golden Vampire Dens. This is California's Gold!

I really needed my notebook, but had no idea where I'd left my purse. "I'll warn you, I have no clue what you're talking about. But I do know two things. This is all very interesting and I want to know everything you can tell me, and you look darn pretty saying it." I smiled and he blushed. Inside, I cheered. I had successfully made him turn a lovely shade of red. "So, if you were Secondus, shouldn't you have taken over instead of Malcolm? Isn't that how it usually works?" Made sense to my mundane sensibility.

"You'd assume, but no. Vampire politics can get a bit dicey and very confusing if you're not involved directly." He spoke a little too openly with me about it all. A man of mystery turned informant. Not likely. There had to be a lot more he was leaving out.

"So, what you're saying is, you aren't allowed to talk about it?" I may be just a dumb girl, but all in all, I was still a snoop. It was my job to dig for the truth. Well, it was before all the pretty vampy boy nonsense crept in and stole my rationality.

"Basically, yes. Since Malcolm invited you personally, you were allowed to attend the summit and of course the masque, but those are all surface events. Nothing of importance happens at those. Nothing the community wouldn't want to be, I don't know, published for the world to see," he said an accusatory tone.

A reporter joke. Nice indirect jab directed right at me. As if I'd run off and set their stories out to print tomorrow. Shit, it'd take at least a few days before I could get it to go to print.

"It's all a face? I see. Now, you've captivated me more than you should have." Dummy.

"I hope no more than I did last night." His smile reminded me of the night before and my vomiting. I dropped my head into my hands and groaned.

"I'm so sorry. If I can make it up..." My voice gave away just how humiliated I truly felt.

He spoke and brought my eyes back to attention. "I can think of so many ways," he said. The smile hadn't left his face; he just talked through it.

A knock at the door tore me away from those gleaming white teeth. "Yes?"

"Hey drunktard! How you feeling?" Tatum strutted into my humble room on bare feet carrying a large glass of orange juice. "Here, drink it."

My eyes turned to slits as I glared at the beautiful blonde who I'd once trusted with my life. The girl who was slowly but surely slipping into the abyss of vampires and red headed freaks. The girl who was dragging me right along with her.

I snatched the glass from her grip and took a big swig. "Gaw! Is this a screw driver?" I asked loudly.

"Yes. Drink it. We need to get ready," she said with a nod.

"For what?" The last thing I wanted to do was get up and go out again. Let alone spend any more time than necessary with the likes of Tatum and her Miracle Whip honey bunny.

"A party, duh." Her facial expression was extreme and pure Tatum. For a split second, I felt like everything was right with the world.

"Didn't we just go to a party?"

"We went to the Masque. Semi-formal. Tonight, Cinderella, you go to a ball!" She raised her arm in the air above her head. "But you must finish your chores before you can go anywhere.

And your first chore is kissing this fine boy here." She leaned over and slung her slender arm around Cyrus's shoulder. "He has been dying to get a hold of that sweet ass for months now. Don't leave him hanging…." she giggled and shifted her eyes to his lower extremities, "or whatever." She moved quickly from the boy and kissed me on the forehead. "Now, get your chores done and get your ass ready. Your chariot arrives in an hour." Tatum's long legs carried her quickly out the door leaving me alone and awkward with Cyrus.

That miniscule Tatum experience was so reminiscent of the good old days, pre-vampire clubs, that it made me hopeful for the future. Maybe Tatum had one last ace up her sleeve to redeem our ever-failing relationship.

"So, do you guys ever stop partying?" I asked with my eyes trained on the fancy bedspread.

"Not usually. For the most part, they see no need." I caught a shrug from the corner of my eye.

"Who? Malcolm?" I asked, sniffing at the glass of orange death Tatum had handed me.

"And the others. Most of the guests at the Masque are fledglings, followers, that sort. But, as far as the elders go—Malcolm, Marienne, and the others—they all have business ventures that allow them to live quite… freely. What else do you do with your time when all that's required of you is to sustain your own life? Eat, drink, be merry."

"Fuckin', fightin', all that," I replied in my best cockney accent.

"Yeah, all that." He caught the reference and chuckled.

I blushed at the thought and stood from the bed. Sure, drunk Dylan was all about *getting some*, but sober Dylan was awkward and self-conscious. Not to mention the fact that I felt so damned on edge in the house of Dracula and all I really wanted to do was look under the stairs for that door.

"I should probably get ready. I doubt there's any way I'll be getting out of going out tonight. Scary witch bitches or no, Tatum will take me by force. Besides, I really would rather not stay in this house all night by myself. Jeez, there isn't even a TV in here," I said trying to cover for the thoughts that danced in my head.

"Malcolm would not allow me to stay here with you, or that would be our Saturday evening."

A stupid look spread across my face and butterflies shot up into my chest. Without thinking about it, a nervous, and kind of creepy, laugh fluttered from my lips. "Well," I started with a tone that was a bit too high-pitched and swallowed it back, "what the hell am I supposed to wear?"

"Formal. Most will be in Victorian garb." He stopped talking and his expression dropped. "You didn't bring anything?" His voice told me he was a bit concerned over my lack of preparation.

"No. I wasn't aware of any of the events this weekend. I packed like I was going on vacation. And one generally does not bring a full Victorian gown as a carry-on."

His brow creased in the center. "Well, I'm not sure then. Unless, maybe…." He trailed off as he got up from the edge of the bed.

Cyrus walked to the beautiful armoire that stood in the other corner. I noticed the gray and blue striped pajama pants he'd been wearing. They flopped around his bare feet as he moved so confidently across the room. I stood there like an idiot and watched him open both doors to the cherry wood cabinet.

"Ah. Here you are." He pulled a wooden hanger covered in

lace and frills from the cabinet. All pink and black.

"Borrow a dress from someone else's stash? Not my style. Besides, I'm not your average bear. My big ass will never fit into that." I shook my head vehemently protesting.

"Hmm. Well, then who's this for?" He pulled a scrawled note from the hook of the hanger and handed it to me. Cyrus stood stone still and quiet while I read the words on the parchment paper.

Dylan,

A sexy gown for the minx I know is hidden within you. Release your inhibitions and have some fun for once. Your beauty will shine if you let it. I love you more than you know.

Yours, Tatum

I didn't know what to say. The ace up her sleeve? I'd been so pissed at her for the way she'd been acting then she went off and totally redeemed herself. Sort of. Not letting me embarrass myself was kind of her thing. And to have had an awesome and likely expensive costume hidden in my room, for Lord knew how long, was very much in the style of Tatum Price. I knew in there somewhere she loved me and I loved her too. Even if she was a cunt bitch whore.

"You sneaky monkey. How long has that been there?" I asked Cyrus.

"A while." He stepped closer and handed me the hanger. "Get ready." He leaned forward and caught me off-guard with a kiss on my forehead. "I cannot wait to see it on you."

Without another word, he left me alone in my room without a view. Being alone for the first time in over a full day allowed my brain to actually process all that I'd absorbed in the events of my Friday night. My purse sat on the dresser beside the cabinet. I snatched my notebook from it and jotted down bullet points as quickly as my hand would allow.

Cyrus was the second in command for the House of whatever in Los Angeles, there were headless bitches all over the United States, a wicked voodoo queen was out for my head, and I puked on an extremely hot vampire boy.

What in the fuck is happening to my life?

Why, suddenly, did I know there was a lifestyle vampire hierarchy, and how in the fuck did I end up in such a compromising position with one of them? There were some fan girls who would pay good money to end up in my situation. Unfortunately for some, my vampy boys were not immortal. Or sparkly. They were on the other hand, annoying, bossy, sexy, and likely pretty dangerous. Aside from the whole living forever thing, they were pretty true to form.

Coffins in the basement? Yet to be confirmed. But I had to say, if my dream of dead things in the basement of the house of Dracula came to fruition, I swore I was done with the whole mess of them. If only to save my own skin.

Since when did I become little miss premonition?

THIRTEEN

MY NEWLY ACQUIRED BALL GOWN, IF YOU COULD CALL IT that, showed off a lot more skin than I would have ever intended on showing. I didn't even show off that much in a bathing suit. If I ever put one on. The top-half consisted of a faux sheer corset, lacing up my back from the top of my ass. A shrug went over the top with sleeves that ended in oversized ruffles. The skirt was mostly open in the front and showed off my short, stocking clad legs complete with pink garter. It was bustled and made my ass look bigger than it actually was and I wasn't exactly happy with that. Other than looking like a massive slut, the costume was pretty killer. I forced myself to relax and figured there would never be another occasion in which I would ever be able to wear it, so I'd better suck it up and have fun.

"So sick." Tatum burst into the room without warning and made me jump.

The sight of her caused a flurry of mixed emotions to flutter around in my head. I hadn't talked to her at length the majority of the trip and had so much to say it hurt my tongue to keep it well bitten.

"Thank you so much. I had no idea I'd need something like this. I love it, but did you really have to make it so… little?" I snarled at my own reflection and checked out my awesome rack in the full mirror that should've been a window.

Tatum was quiet for a minute before she said, "Hmm, well, it looks really great on you." Her reflection in the mirror over my shoulder showed a wrinkle in the center of her neatly plucked eyebrows.

"Really? I feel like a cow." I did feel a bit like a sausage crammed in the corset, but I knew it wasn't as bad as my ego made it out to be.

"Let me tighten those lacings for you." She set her huge makeup case on the dresser and came to me.

"Oh, yeah, that's what I need to be… umph… oh… ah… uck." Tatum pulled and tugged at the ribbon that held me in that sexy device of torture. "Well, at least I know I won't be eating anything tonight. Or, breathing." I checked the mirror one last time and was astonished at the size of my waistline. Fuck breathing, skinny beat oxygen any day.

Tatum didn't talk much after that. She grabbed her makeup bag and started away at my face. Powder puffs and pointed pencils swiped across my eyes. Thankfully, she was tall enough to work on me standing up. I doubted I'd be able to sit down strapped into that corset the way I was. I was kind of glad she'd told me to keep my mouth shut while she worked. It was likely something inappropriate would've come out and she'd jab me in the eye with a pencil.

Tatum was cinched into her corseted dress too. She just had less to squeeze into it. All black, floor length, and high collared, Tatum's gown was more authentic than mine and so not her style at all. I really liked the pin striping on the fabric, but the lack of cleavage threw me.

"What gives? Why am I dressed up like I'm headed off to Moulin Rouge and you look like your auditioning for Gothic Mary Poppins?" I asked during a gap in sharp objects.

"I'm attached," she said with a shrug and went back to work. "You, my darling, haven't had a good dicking in a long while. You need titties. I don't." Tatum moved her lips, but never adjusted her hands as they swiped makeup across my face.

"So, what you're saying is, Malcolm picked it out?" I regretted being snotty right after I said it.

Word of advice: never talk shit to the guy holding sharp objects to your eye. Just saying.

She didn't stop her work. "Yes. It matches his. Being *his,* I need to dress similarly. It's kind of a tradition thing."

His? What has become of my friend? The girl who nailed Cyrus square in the nose just to shut him up.

Breathing a sigh of relief she didn't jab me good in the eye, I said, "Isn't that a little high school?"

"Ha, wait until you see what Cyrus is wearing," she laughed and continued her swoops over my face.

"Why? Why would I care?" I asked, as if I truly didn't. Secretly, I hoped he'd be wearing… nothing. Never mind.

"You care, don't act like you don't. And really, you should, you're his escort. He has to match you." Her brows raised and she laughed through her nose.

"Pink lace? Why in the fuck would you pick pink lace if you knew we'd have to match?" I didn't mind pink on a guy, but I hated to be the reason the poor thing was stuck in pink for the night. Images of him in a frilly lace corset flashed through my head and a whole *Rocky Horror Picture Show* scene took over.

Tatum furrowed her brows. "Me? Why—".

"What a lovely sight," Malcolm said from the doorway, breaking Tatum's concentration.

Cyrus stood behind the red-haired walking dildo, peering over his shoulder. Tatum turned from me and blushed at her suitor. I threw up in my mouth a bit and rolled my eyes. I hoped she'd finished her job because I figured she'd ditch me for her man in no time. I was right.

"Are we ready?" she asked with a giddy smile. She was a totally different person around him. Like he had some kind of power over her. Vampire pixie dust or some shit. The weekend was proving to be all about power. Who had it, who didn't. Who wanted it, who didn't give a fuck. That'd be me. I was a firm believer in never relinquishing control to anyone. Others could only have power over you if you allowed it to happen. So I just… didn't. I wished others could do the same.

"You look amazing, Ms. Hart." Cyrus moved past the two idiots in black on black pin stripes and into the room toward me.

Looking at his perfect face, I cringed in preparation of seeing the thin red line of a recent injury. An injury I'd caused. But there was nothing to be found. He'd been bleeding profusely only an hour ago and there was nothing to show of my handy work.

Maybe it isn't as bad as all that?

Ha! Maybe he's a goddamned vampire you fucking idiot!

Shut up inner-Dylan. You're out of your element.

He wore pink to match mine—sans a lace corset—and he made that shit look good. Head-to-toe black Victorian garb. Down to the pink ascot and spats on his shoes. If it was anyone else, I'd have laughed it was so over the top, but Cyrus could have walked in wearing clown shoes and it would've looked pretty damn good. The only thing he was missing was a silk top hat.

"How do I look?" He flipped a black silk hat in his left hand and put it on his head.

There it is. Now I might laugh.

Why isn't your lip fucked? "Don't you feel ridiculous?" I asked, avoiding the subject that ran rampant through my thoughts, although feeling absurd myself. At some point, I would get to the bottom of all their vampire bullshit. Really, I would.

"It's Halloween, Dylan. Don't you like a good costume party?" He flashed a set of shiny white teeth and his eyes shimmered away. If they could bottle that charm and market it, Cyrus would've been swimming in cash.

"Oh, I guess you're right. It is Halloween. All of this vampire shit made me forget there was an actual reason for all this insanity." I laughed off my own idiocy and shook my head. "So, do you think my new *best friend* will be in attendance?"

"I don't think so. She performs at the Masque every year, but she isn't welcome at the ball. Tonight is for VIP guests only, for the most part. As long as you stay with me, you will be safe until we can get you back home." He smiled a natural and caring smile. I doubted he showed that bad boy off to just anybody.

"We'll meet you downstairs," Tatum called from the

doorway on her way out.

"Well, that visit was short-lived." My brows rose with sarcastic annoyance.

"Hmm, well, it won't matter what those two choose to do with their evening. Tonight, my darling Dylan, I believe you belong to me." He wriggled his eyebrows up and down. "I do hope that won't be a problem."

Better than a poke in the eye with a sharp stick. Shit, better than anything else that could feasibly be happening.

"I think we can make that work." It was my turn to sparkle with charm. Or at least drool charm.

"Well then, I'll leave you to finish up." Cyrus pulled my hand to his lips and pressed a kiss to my knuckles. It wasn't the first time a vampy boy had kissed my hand, but it was the first time a vampy boy donning a silk top hat and tailed coat had.

If my life could choose if it was going to be smooth or rocky, that'd be great.

The door closed gently and I was alone in my room again, hopefully for the last time until I was in my own room, in my own house, in my own damn town. Tatum had laced me, prepped me, spackled me, and now I was as sexy as I could be. Honest.

I grabbed my small purse and tossed my necessities in it. Forcing one last look in the mirror, I moved my heeled boots toward the mirror that should've been a window. The heavy gold frame that surrounded the obviously aged glass was adorned with intricate carvings of nude females wrapped haphazardly in thin cloth. I hadn't really noticed the design before, but I supposed I had intentionally avoided my own reflection during my previous visits to the mirror. I stepped closer to the frame and took a good look at the naked ladies. Each seemed to have their own intentions and seemingly their own personality. One woman carried a clay jar, another balanced a basket of fruit on her head, and yet another held a large circular symbol of some kind. The women were scattered in a sea of roses and grapes on either side trailing up to the top of the frame. There, at the apex of it all, sat another woman. Seemingly singular in her mission and the obvious center of the scene, the woman sat atop a throne of roses and flowing cloth. Her chest was bare proving it was in fact a woman, but the head donned a set of horns and a snout as a bull would have. A disturbing and odd ornament for a mirror frame, but oddly enough, not the strangest thing I'd seen in a day. I made the mental note to ask Cyrus the next time he was alone in my room with me. Which I planned would be mere hours away.

Momentarily satisfied with my inspection of the mirror, I finally looked at my own reflection. There before me stood a pretty, much thinner, gothic version of me. Tatum had done an excellent job of transforming my usual frumpy self into something that could pass for the escort of the Secondus of the House of Idiot Ginger Vamps.

"Hmm, not bad," I said to my reflection as I turned in each direction to get an idea of the full picture.

My chest bulged upward damn near into my chin, creating a deep cavernous cleavage I could've held a beer with. Tatum had left a beaded choker on my dresser to wear if I wanted to, but I thought an exposed neck was sexier.

I blinked my eyes and looked at myself again. In the mirror, it looked like there was a red line around my neck. I rubbed away at it, but it didn't wipe from the glass. Having no clue how I'd have gotten red stuff on my neck I licked my finger and rubbed it along the stain on my skin. To my surprise it smeared into thin smudges along my throat. The more I wiped, the more the red line grew—thicker and thicker—until finally, drips of red poured from it at various points.

My breathing came in heavy pants, nearing the point of erratic. Somehow, with absolutely zero antecedents, my throat had been slit open and was spilling blood into the beautiful plunge of my breasts. Pale skin looked like bloody snow against the stark red of the supposed blood. Hysterically, I tore at my neck trying desperately to stop the red liquid from oozing. After a few seconds, the blood began pumping out like milk from an overturned jug. A glugging noise gurgled from my throat as I stood watching myself bleed to death from a phantom wound. My small hands clamped frantically to my ever-bleeding neck. I stumbled backward toward my pink and gold bed. My weak legs almost toppled unto the bed and gave up, but my will to survive shoved them into gear. I spun away from the view of the mirror and stumbled toward the door in hopes of finding help before it was too late.

My feet tripped over themselves, as they tended to do, and I fell hard to the floor. Out of sheer muscle memory, my hands left the guzzling wound at my neck and reached out to catch my fall. In that moment, I caught the sight of my pale white hands. They were clean, slender fingers and painted nails free of the gore they should've been bathed in. My senses returned to me and I took that instant to analyze the situation. My hands showed no signs of having been covered in blood. I looked down to my bulging chest and saw no red streaks trailing down into my corset top. Confused and bewildered, I crawled back toward the mirror. My brain refused to accept what it saw. There, in the mirror, was me. The pretty, much thinner, gothic, blood-free version of me. No slice along the flesh of my neck. No blood trails down my cleavage.

"What in the actual fuck?" I exclaimed through ragged breaths.

I sat on the floor in my amazing ball gown and wondered why in the fuck I wasn't covered in blood. Or shit, why I wasn't dead. But most importantly, when I'd finally dropped off the deep end into sheer psychosis.

Through the fog of unbridled confusion, I heard my phone ding letting me know I had a message. Brought back to reality, if only momentarily, I reached toward my dropped purse and pulled out my phone. My shaking hands fumbled with the buttons before I saw that Mike had sent me a photo. Out of a need for human interaction, I checked the message. I was horrified to see what came through. He'd been tasteful about it, but it still wasn't what I needed to see in that moment.

The photo depicted the chest of a woman with a large bit of wood protruding from the center of it. I couldn't see the head region, thanks to Mike's excellent camera angle, but I knew there was likely nothing to be seen. Other than the bloody stump that was likely left behind. The focal point of the photo was of a tattoo just to the left of the wooden stake. I was still horribly shaken by my momentary loss of reality, but I was certain I'd seen that tattoo before. Not in that placement, but I'd seen the symbol.

The text with the photo read, *Any ideas?* He was looking for my help. I hated to even put myself into that headless mess, but I actually knew where I'd seen that symbol before, and the fact that it belonged to someone missing their head scared the living shit out of me. Against everything I'd stood for twenty-four hours before, I called Mike.

The other line rang and I took a deep, shaky breath and let it out as slow as I could.

"That was fast," Mike's voice came over the line and I nearly broke down in tears. Not that hearing his voice made me sad. His voice, him in general, held a deep seeded role of protection in my brain. I knew I could never tell him what had just happened. Fuck, he'd have the white coats there in a heartbeat to haul me off to the nut house. Nope, he would never know what had happened. At that point, I didn't think anyone would ever know. That was all I needed, the girl who offed two vampire boys nuts up in the House of Porte, vampire haven, in New Orleans covered in imaginary blood pouring from a fantastical wound. Nope. I'd keep my crazy to myself, thank you very much.

"Mike," I said finally, my voice sounded terrible and I knew he'd pick up on it. Without letting him question me, I continued. "I know that symbol. I can't talk, but I wanted to let you know it's not a vampire thing." I took another deep breath in and let it out without alerting the cop on the other line I was trying to maintain my composure. "It's a voodoo thing."

Saying it out loud, I felt like an idiot. Even knowing with damn near one hundred percent certainty the tattoo on the staked, and presumably headless, girl in the photo was the same I'd seen on the sign at the voodoo shop of horrors.

"How do you know that?" he asked too inquisitively. He trusted my insider information most of the time so I was sure he was trying to get out personal information more than evidentiary material.

"I just do. And yes, I'm certain. You might be looking on the wrong end of the occult spectrum. I gotta go. But you should know, whatever you have to do to find these people, don't forget they really truly believe in everything they're doing and will do anything they can to achieve their fictional power. Good luck."

I heard him start to talk, to question me and everything I'd ever said or done in my entire life, but I didn't have the time or the emotional wherewithal to deal with it, so I hung up without another word. I sat on the floor clutching my phone in my hand, when my door opened and a lovely man stepped through it.

"And how, in the world, did you end up on the floor in that amazing gown?" He stood in the doorway with his hands on either hip like a mother would do.

Not another word escaped his lips before he came and swooped me up from the floor and onto my feet. I was standing before I knew it and on surprisingly stable legs. I didn't know how he did it, but just his presence seemed to make me forget about how horrid life could be.

"Are you alright?" Cyrus asked with caring eyes.

I let myself get lost in the shimmering green that lay between his thick, black lashes for a moment before I answered him. "Better now." The only halfway sane response I could muster after all that insanity I'd encountered.

"Are you certain? I have a feeling there is something you're holding inside." His brows drew together and he peered into my face in search of my hidden thoughts.

"Just an interesting few days. Lots of stuff to put down on paper." He wasn't buying it. "You know, for the book." His eyes narrowed and I felt his unwavering concern burrow into my conscience. "Detective Petersen is having some problems with a case. He needed my help with it and it shook me up a little is all. I'm fine." I smiled the best I could and tried to step around him.

His strong hands held my arms not allowing me to pass. "That's not like you. Must be a terrible case." His voice held so much distrust, I could feel it tickle along my skin leaving behind an eerie sense of guilt.

"Yes, terrible. Not something I'm interested in helping him with further either, so I hope he's able to close it on his own."

"Likewise. I'd hate to know what could've gotten the likes of big tough Dylan Hart frazzled."

"Just more graphic than I was prepared for. I'm sure he has it all under control."

"Were you able to assist him in his… needs?" he asked, as if he thought perhaps I had something going on the side with Mike.

"I answered his question. I hope it helps the case," I responded bluntly. I didn't do well with intrusive boys. Even sexy would-be vampire boys with a death grip on my tender arms.

"Yes." His grip loosened and his eyes softened their gaze. "Well, shall we? Our car is waiting."

I didn't say anything more. Cyrus offered me his arm and I took it cordially. After all that had happened, I really wasn't in the partying mood, but it would've seemed out of sorts if I were to opt out of the big to-do and stay behind all alone in that big creepy house. Although, staying behind would've given me the opportunity to check under the stairs. If there even was an under-the-stairs. I hadn't noticed a door there before, so Lord knew if it was even real. The thought crossed my mind, but I ditched the idea quickly when I thought of being alone in that house with my phantom blood loss. Whatever it was, it scared me, and I wasn't about to stick around and find out if it would happen again. Shit, for all I knew, it was that creepy fucking mirror that was the culprit all along. Not me. Not crazy ol' Dylan. Nope, the haunted mirror did it.

We were feet from the front doors when I decided to drop my bag. The purse fell and coincidently slid toward the foot of the stairs. I let out a fake sigh and moved away to grab it from its convenient position near the area where there should have been a door visible on the side of the staircase. As nonchalantly as I could, I leaned over, stopping all breathing on my part by way of synched corset, and slid my eyes upward toward the side of the stairs. If I could have breathed, it would have been a gasp. There, just as in my dream, a small door sat closed tight under the stairs. At least I'd confirmed there was even a door there in the first place. So, in theory, there was a chance there were also rows and rows of shiny wood coffins hidden down there too.

Fuck ghost hunting. I'm huntin' vampire.

FOURTEEN

TRYING MY HARDEST TO PUT THE BLOODY EVENT OF MY psychotic break behind me, I rode quietly in the back of a shiny black Rolls Royce. A 1930s model if I were to guess. I didn't know much, but what I did know was always random and likely learned from television. Or stalking. Some stuff I learned from stalking.

Something in my subconscious kept making my hand linger to my phantom wound. Checking for thick, warm blood. Nothing. The drive lasted just over twenty minutes and of the dozen times I checked, there was never a sign I was bleeding. I knew I probably looked really stupid with my little dance, but it was like a tick, I just couldn't stop. I snickered softly to myself when I figured, if I were bleeding from a hole in my throat, the two Sanguinarians I was in the car with would likely alert me by kindly cleaning it up with their mouths. The laugh faded to a sinful grin when the image in my head became Cyrus cleaning my bloody mess up with his mouth.

Forget about your sin, give the audience a grin. Always look on the bright side of life...or death.

The song played out in my head as we drove and my fear lifted a little. I'd always been the type to let shit roll off, never really letting anything sway me either way, just kept pushing on. I thanked years of therapy for that one. But it felt like recently, I'd allowed all the macabre that surrounded my life to soak in and change my way of thinking, of reacting toward situations. Apparently, brutally killing two people could have a negative effect on someone. It was natural after all. But my whistle through it and hey, fuck you, guys attitude seemed to be the most affected. Why else would I have been hallucinating ethereal injuries if my thick candy coating was up and running? Nothing should've been penetrating it and causing quite that reaction.

I do have a history of being given hallucinogens in the presence of these bloodsucking freaks. Maybe it really isn't me after all.

"Here we are." The Irish accent of the asshole driver brought me from my thoughts to the present.

Our car pulled through a set of wrought iron gates that seemed to open on their own. A southern spectral perhaps? We were in the mecca of haunted shit, but I doubted it. Motorized gates were a much more likely scenario.

A long sweeping drive slung us from the street to the valet directly in front of the few steps leading to the entrance. All outward appearances told me the building was probably once a house. Like the one we were spending the weekend in, only bigger and marginally less creepy.

My door opened and a solemn man in a fancy hat stood somber-faced, holding it open for me. My heeled-boot held strong as I slid out of the car as smoothly as I could under the pressure of my corset. Cyrus took the place of the man in the hat and again held his arm out for me. Such a gentleman. It seemed to be a new development during our weekend getaway. He never really struck me as the old-fashioned type before, but then again, I really didn't know him that well. From my experience, people tended to surprise you and throw a curveball when you were least expecting it.

The two of us waited for his Primus to retrieve *his* lady from the passenger seat and lead us inside. I had discovered quickly that nothing was done without the head guy doing it first. In our case, that was Malcolm. I really hadn't had the chance to get to know any of the other Primus… es? Primusi? I didn't know any of the other head honchos so I didn't have anything to compare it to within the bizarre blood-drinking culture, but in my opinion, he took his seat of power a little too literally.

Two tough guys stood on either side of the double doors. They looked armed and were likely off-duty cops. Or rotten ex-cops looking for work. That was how they paid the bills, moonlighting. Seemed a bit overkill on the security, but judging by my need to be at least temporarily protected, I was not about to pitch a fit. I was more than happy to leave those gun-wielding commandos to their duties as long as that meant they were keeping out vicious little voodoo mamas with the rest of the riffraff.

Malcolm stopped at the entrance and waited for the doors to open. The two bouncers stood at their posts as if they were the royal guard. I was actually half expecting their duties to extend to opening doors, but I was dead wrong. Instead of instantly being allowed in, our foursome stood on the large white porch in succession, waiting like losers.

Finally, the doors opened from the inside out, and two staff members stood at each. They wore what one could assume to be traditional Victorian garb. Black on white, spats, coat tails, the works. No hats. Just discretely combed hair pulled back into ponytails at the nape of their neck. At first, I thought it odd that two men would have hair long enough to put in a ponytail, but then I realized one was a woman. Dressed as a man, she nearly mirrored the man on the other door. Maybe they were siblings, I didn't know. In any other circle, I'd have asked. I'd learned my lesson never to ask more than you were willing to pay for with a pound of flesh. Or a bucket of blood. Who knew a group of basement-dwelling pale faces could ever be so damn creepy if given the proper tools to survive in society. Thank you, modern media.

Granted they were not above the law. Let's face it, they weren't celebrities or anything. Those types of people might still be stuck rocking role-playing games in their parents' basements had there not been a serious shift in social acceptance thanks to pop culture. They afforded grand masques and public social events where youngsters flocked in droves and spent their parents' hard-earned money for a moment in the life of a bloodsucking fiend from beyond the grave. Or mommy's basement.

As had occurred once before at the summit in the teahouse, a hostess greeted us at the door and took our names. She escorted our party to yet another set of doors where another hostess met us and detained us in a holding pattern until she was able to open the door with zeal and introduce us all properly.

"Presenting, Master Malcolm McTavish." *Say that five times fast.* "Primus, House of Cailleadh and escort, Mistress Tatum Price."

The two pranced into the beautifully decorated ballroom making eye contact with as many guests as they could on their way.

"Presenting, Sir Cyrus Atossa, Secondus, House of Cailleadh and escort, Mistress Dylan Hart."

It was our turn to make our grand entrance. Firmly attached to his arm, Cyrus and I stepped into the oversized ballroom with what felt like a hundred eyes on us. Some looked at me with a disappointed glare. Others smiled and seemed to approve of the two of us together. I spotted Dominika seated with Marienne at a table near the back. Neither acknowledged our eye contact. Most of the guests, mostly the girls, just stared at sexy Cyrus in his fancy costume. I was fine with that. I knew, unlike our first meeting and the others that followed, I was likely going to spend the rest of my weekend with him. I was also becoming strangely aware of the feeling I was being pranced around like a steer at auction. I had been stuck in my own thoughts, as I usually was, while Cyrus led me around the innermost section of the shiny wood dance floor.

I noticed the looks from the guests when we first entered, but there was no reason for them to continue watching. A thought flew through my slow brain. It was possible the weekend was some sort of setup. Judging by what I knew of Tatum, I was fairly certain she played a major role in it. If it were true. Malcolm hated me as much as I hated him, so I doubted greatly my presence was any of his doing. That left Cyrus himself. What motive would he have had to ask me to be his escort on our strange vacation? Tatum had been the one who originally invited me along. She even insisted with all her might that I come, even as I vehemently protested. I might've been dumb. I wasn't stupid. Yeah. I wasn't exactly thrilled about the idea, no matter how much research it would prove to offer. But it was Tatum who originally convinced me I needed it for my health and my soon-to-be work of fiction. Not to mention how strongly she'd assured me I'd be tagging along to keep her company only to leave me hanging with the sexy Secondus for the weekend.

Cyrus had coincidently been forced to retrieve me and all my shit from my place on our way to the airport. My room was placed directly across the hall from his. Our outfits were obviously an intentional and well thought out coordinated set. It was a big job, even for the likes of Tatum Price. There was absolutely no conscious reason I could find that would cause Cyrus to be the mastermind behind those shenanigans. Hell, I shot the man and hadn't spoken to him in five months. No man, no matter how hard up, waited around for a girl for five months. It just wasn't done.

Unless that man is Michael Petersen.

Our rotation was finally over, and Cyrus led his cow to her seat. I felt a skeptical expression set in on my face as I took a seat in a linen-covered chair at a well-set table. Centerpieces stood elegantly with reaching, white branches jutting from tall, fluted crystal vases. All of the linen was a matching white, making it all look like winter with the sparkling crystal. The only light came from the hundreds of deep red, tapered candles perched atop each table in dramatic crystal candelabras. Red roses stuck deliberately from the tops of each fluted vase making it look as though the white branches were growing from pools of blood. If it weren't for the obvious vampire presence, I'd have thought I was at a wedding. A fantastically decorated wedding at that.

Trying hard to keep my mind from flipping back to the horrific incident in my room with the blood and all, I decided to direct my energy to finding out why I was being pranced around the room like cattle at auction. Cyrus took his seat beside me, and I waited a moment for him to get nice and settled. It seemed the rest of the guests were seated at tables with their respective Houses, mostly the higher-ups and a few others I didn't really recognize from the summit at the tea house. Each round table sat about eight people, all of which were dressed in the same melodramatic corresponding Victorian inspired garb. Malcolm and Tatum were sitting a few seats away from us, but sharing our eight-seat table. Apparently, we would be joined by four more guests. Wonderful.

"So," I began, "I need to ask you something. I'm just going to be blunt about it." As if there were any other way? "And I'm going to expect you to be honest with me. Please know I am fully prepared to beat the shit out of you at any given moment so choose your words wisely." I paused for a moment to allow Cyrus a chance to acknowledge he heard and understood my words. He looked blankly into my eyes and nodded. "Good. Why am I here?" I'd kept my voice lower than my average boisterous tone out of respect for the other guests who were all engaged in their own tightknit conversations, but I minced no words.

"On this earth? Or in this room?" Cyrus asked, avoiding the original question and in turn lighting a fire under my ass that had before only been a stack of kindling.

"Why am I along for this bloody strange ride? Aside from Tatum being here, I see no reason to be asked along. None that make sense to my vampire-ignorant mind anyway. I was hoping you could enlighten me." Taking the chance at being seduced by those perfect emerald eyes, I glared into them, trying to elicit fear in the gorgeous man. I doubted it worked, but he did start talking.

"I asked Tatum to invite you," his voice was low and rumbling and as sincere as I could imagine him to sound.

In the end, he and I weren't all *that* familiar with each other. Not in that sense anyhow. It seemed a camaraderie had been building out of necessity and fear of being lonely, but if it weren't for our vampire weekend, it was likely I would have continued living my life trying to avoid his existence as I had the five months we didn't speak in the first place. When you'd shot a guy and put him in the hospital for a week, you had the right to assume there would never be a real relationship there. Also, aside from desperately wanting to see what he had hidden under those lovely man panties, I really had little interest in an honest to goodness boyfriend-girlfriend thing. And a part of me presumed he was the type to not put too much stock in relationships as well.

"Why?" Always good to know the intentions of others. In sexually tense situations, it could be easy to forget that everyone had a motive. What that motive was defined the good guys from the bad guys.

"I wanted to see you."

Oh. Is that all? Come on, cockle-pus, I wasn't born yesterday.

"You can't call a bitch up on the telephone? A text? A fucking homing pigeon? Was it necessary to bring me all the way here to have a conversation?"

"Alright," he huffed. "Primus and Secondus are required to bring an escort to the Masque. These public events are not for us. They are a way to integrate into society and allow our culture to show they are not the dangerous child stealing freaks the media makes them out to be. If we, as the hierarchy, appear to live normal lives. Have dates…" He ran a hand over mine and I jerked it away. "Tonight is for our community only, I chose you as an escort. This is not a requirement. It is my choice." He touched my hand again and I let him. If only for vanity. A traditionally dressed waitress appeared with a cloth-wrapped bottle and poured bubbly champagne into expensive looking flutes.

"And what of the public? So far I have attended one public event. Not exactly the mecca of vampire culture. More like a nightclub." Like the few I'd already been familiar with.

"Later, after we have established our routines, the event will broaden to select guests."

"The ones who bought their way in?"

"The guests we are to welcome have purchased a ticket to attend, yes."

"What about the summit at the tea house? Why was I there?" I wanted to know everything.

"Because I wanted you there." His eyes softened and looked at me until I had to adjust my gaze to the tip of his nose. Just being safe. "That escort is reserved for significant others. Usually donors, but not always. Malcolm brought Tatum because their intentions toward one another are long term."

I wasn't sure how to take that statement. Not only had he confirmed that Tatum and Malcolm had no plans to split and in fact had become some kind of Herman and Lily. Only not even close to as cool as those two. He'd basically said he dragged me along to an event where the guys only brought the extra special girlfriends. In guy code, that was a big deal. I wasn't ready for a big deal.

"What would you have done if I had told Tatum no?" It was

a totally valid question and not cheeky in the least. Really.

A sinful smile spread across his lovely face. "I would have compelled you." His hand squeezed mine sensually then released it to rest lonely on the table. What a tease.

"So, really, I'm here because of you? Not Tatum." The roller coaster of emotions that girl had me on was beginning to get old, and I wanted off.

"It was a collaborative effort. But if I hadn't wanted you to be here, it's likely you wouldn't be. Not of Tatum's will. Of mine. You are here, darling Dylan, because I honestly could not have considered a better partner for the weekend. Simple." He laughed softly and broke his gaze.

Well, how 'bout that.

"And what about the last five months? Other people… I mean *things* on your mind? Seems a little off to wait around for little ol' me." Cynical and suspicious until the bitter end.

"Sometimes, it takes a man a little longer to sort out the connection between his brain and his dick." He used the word flippantly and it seemed out of character. "It is of no fault of the woman on the waiting end of the game. I blame God for tangling up the line." He smiled like he was talking to one of his oldest friends; innocent and comfortable and completely honest. If there was anything I appreciated in the world, it was honesty.

Mostly satisfied with his answer, I let it go. Not really because I didn't want him to explain it down to the last detail, but it seemed as though they wanted everyone to be quiet and focus their attention to the dance floor. I let out a long sigh and grabbed hold of the narrow stem on my champagne flute. A tasty looking strawberry lay at the bottom of the delicious bubbly goodness waiting for me to gobble it up. I smiled at my own absurdity and took a hearty sip. No one, ever, guzzles champagne. It'd shoot right out your nose if you weren't careful. And let's face it, if you got to the point you were guzzling the bubbly stuff, there was no way on this earth you were worried about being cautious of carbonated explosions in your nasal cavity. Word to the wise, you shouldn't do it. Want to guzzle? Grab a beer.

A public service announcement brought to you by Dylan Hart.

I enjoyed the sensation of tickling bubbles popping their way down my gullet before I sat the glass down on the stark white linen. My eyes fell on my hand in an unconscious drift.

"Oh," I gasped softly but caught it before it escalated.

I blinked my eyes tight and looked again. Dainty drops of red liquid fell from my wrist to the white cloth on the table. I stared for a long while trying to make certain what I was seeing was real. Reality seemed to have become a fleeting thing. Again, I closed my eyes and tried again to look upon the bleeding mess. Nothing had changed with a few blinks, but my rationale tried to tell me it wasn't actually happening. I wasn't actually bleeding from a ghostly wound in the middle of a lavishly decorated vampire ball.

My hand remained glued to the stem of the flute and I realized someone would notice I was stuck there. Quickly, I retracted my bleeding arm, grabbing my napkin from the table as I did. I shoved my arm into my lap and wrapped it in the white cloth napkin. In the first few seconds, blood began spreading like an ink blot across the threads of the fabric. I could feel my heart speeding up, beating so rapidly I thought it'd jump straight from my chest. I tried so hard to control my breathing. If I were really bleeding, Cyrus would notice and come to my aid. If I wasn't, all my gasping would cause alarm to those around me. Better to be safe than locked in a nuthouse.

My other hand squeezed the affected area with such force I began to lose feeling in the fingers of the bleeding hand. Risking exposure, I loosened my grip and lifted the cloth. I had to see where the blood was coming from. Just below the palm of my hand, a long jagged line stretched up my arm four or five inches. Blood oozed from the wound much slower than that of the fake slice to the throat, but it was still fucking terrifying. And absolutely unrelenting.

"Shit," I whispered to myself as I shoved the cloth against the open cut.

There was no pain. At all. I thought hard through the waves of insanity about the first incident. The bleeding throat in that mirror in my room. I'd assumed it had been the mirror, but obviously there was no mirror present so it must've been something else. I tried to remember if I felt pain while I'd bled out all over that shiny wood floor. It didn't seem like I had, but I really was having a hard time focusing. Pain or not, my body was reacting to the loss of blood as it should. White spots fell over my vision as the lack of oxygen began to sink in. It wouldn't be long before I was flat on the floor. I worked hard at controlling my breathing as I prayed for it to stop. My head swooned and I saw gray spilling into my vision, blocking my sight and letting me know I'd soon be unconscious. My head fell forward and slammed with an audible thwack against the thick wooden table.

"Are you alright?" Cyrus asked in a halfhearted chuckle. Maybe he was trying to sound like nothing was happening to keep me calm. Maybe he had no clue what was happening and thought I'd spaced out and bonked my head on the table. Perhaps, I'd embarrassed him just a bit.

I lifted my head swiftly from the table and flung my arm into view. Nothing. I laid the cloth napkin along my section of the table and examined it for any signs of blood. Nothing. My eyes closed again, this time, in gracious thanks to all that is holy.

"I'm not feeling good. Maybe I need to eat something." Like some robust antipsychotics.

"Would you like to leave? I can have a car take us back."

I didn't doubt that was true, I just wasn't about to make him leave. Nor was I about to be alone with him uninterrupted during the psychosis I was experiencing. More terrifying than actually being crazy was other people knowing about it. I did, however, want to go back to my own home where I could be crazy in peace and figure out what in the fuck was going on. I had a hunch it had something to do with the particularly vivid dream I'd had and all the feelings of my dad coming back up, but I didn't have the time or emotional strength to handle all that. A better choice, in my own kooky head, was to ignore it the best I could and focus on allowing Cyrus to buy me drinks and call me pretty.

All the tables grew quiet and I followed along. Instead of actually answering, I shook my head and looked away. I was fine. No need to have bothered anyone else with my crazy.

"Welcome to all," the rotund man who I'd been on stage at the masquerade, said over a microphone standing in the center of a sparkling dance floor. "Our fifteenth annual Masque de Sang was once again a sensual and eye pleasing event for the ages. On behalf of Marienne and the House of Porte, I thank all who attended. Tonight, I am teased and pleased to introduce this year's entertainment for our first course. Please, I beg of you, open your hearts and your minds to the carnal, the prevailing, the decadent, Madam Azelie."

"You have got to be fucking kidding me." I closed my eyes and threw my head back in frustration.

More terrifying than crazy? That bitch.

FIFTEEN

ENTERING STAGE LEFT, MADAM AZELIE HERSELF, CLAD IN black on black, dripped in gold beading and coins that jingled as she slithered to center stage. The hush that fell over the crowd intensified the eerie vibe that rolled off Azelie's smooth butter-tinged skin. Each foot pointed as her toes touched the slick wooden dance floor with every graceful step. In total unison, her hips swayed gracefully while her arms slinked around her body to a slowly rising beat from an unseen source.

In one hand, she held a long, wavy stick but it didn't seem to serve a purpose. Not that I could see anyway. The bongo beat intensified until Azelie was shaking her body along with the quickened thrumming. Cyrus and I sat at a table three back from the stage. She hadn't seen me yet, as far as I could tell, and I prayed it stayed that way.

"Safe?" I looked at Cyrus and said through my teeth. Either he was a big fat liar or somebody had changed the rules.

"There was no way I could have known she would be our entertainment," he whispered. "I have seen her perform at the Masque many times, but tonight's events usually include entertainment from classic performers. Magicians are common. Always are presented within the Victorian period. This… this makes no sense." He shook his head softly looking at the dancing girl instead of me.

No sense? Obviously someone read their tea leaves wrong, because there she was. Right in fucking front of me, doing her weird dance, playing her mind fuck games.

Like a light bulb had literally clicked on over my head, I decided she had to have been the reason for the phantom wounds. Everything in my head told me it could not be true. Shit like that just did not happen. I was a firm believer in the idea of God and the devil. Good and evil, and all the fuzzy gray shit in between. I'd even given my fantasies over to ghostly spirits and earthly ESP, but witchcraft? That was about as believable as vampires.

I still wasn't certain exactly how she'd done it, but I knew somewhere in my inner intuitive zone that she had. And I was going to kill her for it. Okay, maybe not, but I was sure as hell going to make sure she knew who the fuck she was screwing with.

I decided I was going to give her a taste of her own potion. Turning fully in my chair to face her with my entire body, I adjusted my face to *bitch* and waited for her to notice me. I tried with everything I had to send my hatred toward her, to let her know I knew what she'd done and I was not going to stand for it. It didn't take long.

With a flourish of her layered skirt, she spun facing toward me. Her long dreadlocks had been left down and allowed to hang down to the middle of her back, trinkets and charms dangled sporadically from them. Her piercing blue eyes caught mine and a devious smirk splattered across my face with all the fury I'd held in me for so long. Her brow crooked and a nearly identical smile spread across her face. If the two of us had had a pair of swords, we'd be challenging each other to a duel right about then. Instead, I knew what the look meant. I'd challenged her and she'd accepted. In other words, it was on. And I'd dug myself tits deep into a hole I'd probably not crawl out of in one piece.

I stared, and she stared right back. Her devilish grin flipped in a flash and the wavy stick flew to her mouth. She spat on the end of the plain old stick and it caught fire with a vengeance. I'd seen fire blowers before and never had I seen one start the fire from nothing. Perhaps they had hired a magician after all. A sleight of hand, a little hypnotism, you never could tell what the human mind was capable of until it was challenged in all the right ways. Like someone training themselves to appear, for all intents and purposes, to be all powerful voodoo mama, but in reality, they were just a well-trained illusionist. There were TV specials about that kind of crap. Being a magician was one thing, but honestly believing you were filled with the power of all the gods, or whatever, was fucking crazy. I could handle crazy.

The fire on her wavy stick raged on as she spun it around her body and over her messy locks. Her gaze broke from mine the moment the fire started and had not returned. I would probably prefer she worry about the flaming stick in her hand over starting shit with me. Just for the sake of safety. Death by burning dance hall? Carrie style. Not my thing.

“She seems to not have noticed you,” Cyrus whispered in my ear.

A sick snigger rolled up my chest and into my throat. She’d noticed alright. Secretly, I was planning my attack. Obviously, I could not call her out in the middle of the lovely room filled all of those beautifully dressed people and the gorgeous crystal. I would have to catch her off guard. In a back room perhaps. I would’ve preferred to take Cyrus with me, just in case. But he’d probably try to talk me out of it. We didn’t need any of that. I wanted my day in the mystical sun, and dammit I was going to get it. That bitch didn’t know who she was fucking with. I was fine when she was only trying to intimidate me. Pretending to know things about my life. Even when she stared me down from her spot on the stage at the Masque. But snatching a bitch up by the hair was not okay in the least. And brainwashing said bitch into seeing blood spewing from her body was the last damn straw. The blood she’d drawn was all in my head. The blood I’d draw would likely spew horrifically from hers.

The sensation I’d gotten the moment I jammed that broken piece of pool cue into the soft flesh of Diego was finding a way back into my psyche. Normally, I’d have been terrified of that feeling, but in that moment I welcomed it. I’d felt so beaten down on my trip to the Big Easy, and it was my turn to lash back. I needed that sensation, that feeling of invincibility, if only to keep from being absolutely and totally terrified of big bad voodoo mamas.

She continued her dance across the shiny floor. Firelight from her flaming stick glistened off every surface. Someone dimmed the room lights allowing her fire stick to steal the show. Her dance moved from sensual to seemingly ritualistic. She lifted her feet and stomped them back down in a clear cadence.

Her head lashed back and forth with each stomp, sending her dreads flying, and with it her back arched like a cat. Someone, somewhere, was playing a percussion instrument for her that sounded similar to a set of bongos or a conga drum.

Coins and charms that dangled from the thick band around her hips, jingled away with her movement. The flaming stick, maybe three feet long, seemed to be dancing to its own drummer. She was moving it at its own pace separately from her body.

The audience was enthralled. Each plastic-fanged mouth lay open. Every set of heavily adorned eyes stared with a shiny glaze at the hypnotic woman. Just as I began to feel as though I was also falling into her charms, she bent quickly at the waist, slamming the fire-free end of her wavy stick into the wooden floor with an echoing thwack. The fire on the stick burst into a massive flame for an instant and when it cleared, revealed a snake at her feet. A snake that had not been there previously.

By firelight, I watched the snake, a smaller version of the gigantic albino python she'd had at the Masque, slither its way up her bare leg. Her hands raised high into the air as if she were praising the slithering thing at her feet. Or perhaps thanking something on high for putting it there. A stage hand I was assuming. Hoping.

The flame on her stick began to die down as she stood with her hands to the sky. Her scaly buddy made its way up her thigh and began wrapping itself around her waist. The drum beat thumped again and Azelie lowered her hands to grasp the snake at her waist. Her hips moved, nearly a different entity than her bust as she undulated with the beat.

Her fingers caressed the slick body of the legless beast, but she never actually attempted to move it. Allowing it to make its way up her body, it nearly reached her throat in a matter of a minute. The snake circled her neck but made no attempt at remaining there for good. Instead, it continued up under and through her thick dreads, slithering over her face. Finally, the thing stopped, nestling at the apex of her head in the form of a sadistic crown.

Azelie lifted her fiery stick again and spewed liquid over the small flame that remained. A huge gust of white hot flame shot out away from her face and toward the audience. Gasps came from every corner as the guests stared on in sheer astonishment. Funny, a room full of vampire community hierarchy and that was what amazed them. A girl with a snake and stick.

When the dance resumed, post flaming stick, the snake that once perched on top of those thick dreadlocks appeared as a crude clay crown. Something you would see in a museum, not on a girl dancing with a burning stick in the center of a crowd of lifestyle vampires. The snake had disappeared from our view and it appeared I was not the only one amazed by this. I still burned with the fiery passion of hatred for the woman, but I could recognize talent when I saw it. Terrifying, yes. Pretty damn impressive, you betcha.

Her head swung from side to side as she stomped each foot with the rhythm. The wavy stick still burned, but only a small flame in comparison to the plume of yellow flames I'd seen it produce. The drumbeat sped up again and with it her movement. The clay crown stayed firm on her head through all the whipping of her heavy dreads. Her creamy skin glowed in the firelight and even from three rows back, I could see her nearly iridescent blue eyes. The black that surrounded them, a mask of charcoal makeup, assisted in their glow. The music sped to an almost intolerable speed. Thump, thump, thumping, on and on and on.

My heart fell into its cadence and my lungs dragged in air at a much faster rate than humanly necessary. The beat took over my thoughts to the point all my head could wrap itself around were the thumps coming from the alto drum.

Azelie's movement mimicked the sound in my head and soon my body began moving to match her; a small rocking of my torso from my seat. Even the corset didn't deter my movement. I felt as though I had no control over my own body. Not that I had really tried to stop what I was doing. It was as though some unseen force compelled my body to move with the music. A quick glance around the room proved I was not the only one. Those closest to me were obviously stuck in the same trancelike state I was. Moving with the music to mimic the girl on stage. Her footfalls came faster and faster until I thought my heart would spring from my chest and bounce right into her grubby little hands.

Just as I thought I'd black out from the rapid heart rate, the beat stopped. My heart just about stopped right along with it. In what seemed like only a second, the rhythm changed from a steady beat to a rattling maraca. Azelie spun with the stop of the beat and dropped her head back, her face pointed to the sky. During the transition from steady beat to shakers, she lifted the flaming stick to her upturned face and spit her magic fluid over the small flame. The fire ignited into the largest burst of flame of the evening. Nearly blinding me, and I assumed the rest of the audience. My eyes instinctively blinked against the bright heat and she was gone. Somewhere in the flame, she'd vanished. Stick and all. Left on the floor where her feet had once stood, the larger of her two albino pythons coiled in and over itself.

It took a solid thirty seconds for the crowd to recognize what transpired. As they did, the room was overtaken by uproarious applause. One guest stood. Then another and another. Until Madam Azelie, badass voodoo bitch, and my personal arch nemesis for the weekend, was receiving a hearty standing ovation.

Lace gloves came off dainty fingers to allow proper whistling. Men stood and seemed a bit too excited to have seen the scantily clad blue-eyed witchy woman swinging her hips around the floor. Cyrus began to stand until he caught my glare and firmly planted his ass back into his covered chair. I refused to stand. I could give a shit how it made me appear. I honestly couldn't believe Cyrus had given her the time of day. Apparently, he did care how it made him appear.

I waited for her encore. Waited to see if she'd reappear on a high rafter somewhere proving how magical she truly was. It didn't happen. In fact, as the standing vampire people started to take their seats again, it seemed as though there was a bit of confusion as to what to do with her serpent friend she'd left behind.

She was there somewhere. In a hidden room. Backstage, if there was one. My inner bitch screamed at me to get up and go find the trollop. I'd like to pretend that I knew better than to listen to that bitch. I didn't. In fact, more often than not, my inner bitch was the one who controlled my world.

Speaking softly, I excused myself to the restroom. It should have raised a red flag with my supposed comrade, Tatum. If she were paying any sort of attention, she'd have caught on that I was not behaving like myself. Me, speaking softly? Cyrus nodded questioningly but didn't protest. Tatum's lack of attention dug that knife in just a little deeper.

Out the double doors, I frantically scanned the area. I

searched every nook and cranny for a side entrance to another portion of the house turned banquet hall. When Azelie entered the ballroom, she'd come from a darkened corner to that end of the room. Somewhere, there had to be a way to get backstage from the entryway.

My heeled boots clicked the wood floors as I tromped around on the hunt for a hidden door. On the backside of a set of sweeping stairs, so much more elegant than those in the home I was staying for the weekend, a section was blocked by your average red velvet rope. There must've been no other color option as far as velvet ropes were concerned. Red had the corner on that market. Also, not an impenetrable fortress by any means. Glancing around innocently, checking for passersby, I unhooked the gold hook from its cradle and slipped through. Simple enough.

On the other side of the roped barricade, there wasn't much to be giddy about. A well-camouflaged breaker box that was hidden under the stairs and a door marked private were the only things of interest. The breaker box obviously meant nothing to me, unless I was into dreadful pranks. I wasn't.

The door, which I hoped desperately was unlocked, had been all that I was looking for. One last check for gawkers and I turned the brass knob over. It clicked twice and pulled open freely. Must not have been too important or it would've been locked. The space on the other side was dark, but the ambient light allowed me to make out pipes and scaffolding proving it was likely a backstage entrance of some sort. Or a dark, dank back area where they slaughtered the innocent.

I slipped in as quietly as my boot clad feet would carry me. I was surprised to find the flooring on the other side of the door to be carpeted. I assumed it was intended to not allow the guests to hear everything happening in the background. A staging area I believed they call it. Not really a backstage, but where a bride might hide with her groom before they made their grand entrance for the reception. Or a large birthday cake with a sexy lady inside could've been stowed away until just the right time.

I followed the overhead scaffolding toward what sounded like instrumental music playing. The entertainment was over and the dinner was beginning. Thick cords and ropes were strung up and around the modern metal frames, and I figured it was a new addition to the original home. Kerosene and candlelight could take you only so far until you had to come into the modern century.

My heart fluttered and flipped over itself when I heard something rustling around in the shadows with me. In my head, I thought of all sorts of fantastic things. A voodoo zombie raised from its gravely solitude to wreak havoc on my delicious flesh. Some kind of horrific snake creature summoned by black magic to swallow me whole. Or the badass voodoo mama herself. I couldn't tell where the sound was coming from so I slowed my footsteps until I was at a full stop. All the lace and material that made up my skirt had made almost as much noise as my clicking heels on the wooden floors.

I waited and listened, ears trained on any coming movement. I really didn't have a plan for the moment I came into full face-to-face contact with Azelie. I really hadn't had the chance to confront her before. Not counting the time she ripped a chunk of my hair out. I really didn't have the opportunity to stand my ground with the tiny woman clung to my body like a little spider monkey.

I figured I'd wing it when the chance came available. I had

hoped it didn't come to blows; I really wasn't dressed for that sort of thing. Just my luck, one of my tits would've come popping out of the constricting bodice I was trapped in.

The rustling came again, much closer than before. I froze. My breath ceased in my lungs as I waited for further evidence of impending confrontation. With little noise coming from me, I was able to pick up on the faintest sounds. More obvious noises flowed through the darkened space and the sound of feet shuffling hesitantly across carpeted floor came through. My ears picked up where the steps were coming from and they were moving up directly behind me. I closed my eyes in an attempt to heighten my sense of hearing. In the dark, moving toward me, a set of feet stepped closer to my position. I didn't wait another second. Drumming up all the courage I could, I spun on the balls of my feet to face my shadow in the dark. Clench fists swung with me in an unconscious effort to get the upper hand on the situation. Something grabbed my wrist and stopped it mid-motion.

"What could you possibly be doing snooping around in a darkened hallway?" Cyrus asked in a highly accusatory tone.

The fact that he'd followed me in the first place told me he already knew what I was up to. There would be no other reason for him to try and catch me before I did something stupid.

"Looking for something," I answered, still hoping there was a chance I'd run across my target somewhere in that hall filled with modern theatrical crap.

"You won't find anything worthwhile in here. I'd suggest coming back to the table. They've served dinner and I think you would do well to get something to eat." His perfect speech pattern mixed with the attire made it easy to imagine him in another era. An era that would allow his chivalry to flourish.

Unfortunately for him, it was the twenty-first century, and I was not one for chivalry. Carry my shit, sure, try to impede a serious ass kicking? Not on your fucking life.

"You would do well to get the fuck out of my face." I did my best to stare him down in the dark. Bits of light slipped through, but only enough to not get yourself tangled in cording, not enough to really make an impact with a good stink eye.

"I swear it, Dylan, I will pick you up by your hair and drag you from this place and back to the solitude of your lovely pink room if you do not come with me right now." He tried so hard to sound threatening.

"Ha! I'd love to see that." I scoffed, trying to stay quiet out of respect for the guests on the other side of all the ropes and pipes.

"You have no idea what you're doing. Do you think she will allow you to overpower her? Do you honestly think she's not capable of making everything you hold dear to you a burning pile of ash at her feet?" Ominous, always so damned ominous.

"Alright, that's going too far. She's just a nutty little girl who is pretty damn good at illusion stuff. Shit, someone should give her her own documentary. Six part series. But in no way does she hold any form of 'magical powers.'" Yes, air quotes.

"You are fucking daft woman." In the shadows, I saw his hands lift and shake around his head in frustration. I felt the same way about him.

"Get fucked." Screw respect.

"I've already tried that. Wouldn't want a repeat of last night, now would we?" His voice was sharp and his words cut deep.

That fucker. I knew he wasn't that remarkable. No one, no matter how empathetic, was okay with someone else barfing in their face. Ever. I didn't say anything for a long moment. He seemed the type to enjoy baiting someone into an argument, but would easily back down if the bait wasn't snatched up.

"Listen," he said, finally breaking the silence. "I promise you, with every validity I can provide, Azelie d'Entremonte is not the type of person you want to get yourself intermingled with. I want you to forget there was ever an altercation. Forget you ever made contact with her and I'll take you away from here. We can go anywhere you'd like. I'll take you to see the city. We can tour the cemeteries if you'd like. I noticed your interest in the group tour yesterday. Anything. Really, I just want you to forget Madam Azelie, forget all of this, and make it back home to the safety of your apartment tomorrow night. Please."

"And if I forget? What then? She has been at every function I've attended since I met her. Is this coincidence or is she following me? I don't really see why I'm so goddamned important to her, but isn't odd to turn up in so many aspects of our weekend. Shit, I'm surprised she didn't infiltrate my dreams with her fancy magic." As soon as the words escaped my lips, I realized that was a distinct possibility. Why else would I dream of bloody children and shiny caskets?

How in the holy fuck would that little bitch be able to control my dreams? If that's true, there's nowhere to hide. Nothing I can do, but sit at home and suck cock for Skittles until my head falls right off my shoulders and rolls into her fucking lap.

"No. I don't believe tonight to be a coincidence. I believe, in some form or another, she coerced Marienne to allow her to perform tonight."

Cock-fuckle.

"Why Marienne?" The intricate interworking of vampire hierarchy had become messy. Screw research. True fiction would've been easier to get a handle on than all that bullshit.

"She's our host. She controls every aspect of the event from beginning to end. The Masque, the summit, tonight's vampire ball, and the closing ceremonies tomorrow are all at the hands of our host, Primus of New Orleans. There is no way Azelie could be here without the approval of Marienne." His tone was so serious I waited for portentous music to begin in the background. "I need you to leave with me, now. If she has Marienne convinced she's harmless, there may be no protection for you here. Malcolm is clueless to the situation, and I doubt he'll leave the side of his dear Tatum unless she leaves first." He shook his head in disgust. I agreed with him on that one. Everything else, yeah, fuck that shit.

"Look, I don't believe in that kind of shit. So she's a fucking loon with a thing for fat chicks, who are you to stop me from confronting said loon and nipping that shit in the magical bud?" I tapped my foot and waited for a response.

"Because if you stay here, there is no way I can predict what will happen."

"What's to say this woman won't follow me? Keep following me wherever I go." The thought of that actually scared me. Magical or not, stalking was fucking real and could get pretty damned scary.

"I'm asking you to forget her. Stop thinking of her. Pretend as if she doesn't exist."

"What, is that the antidote?" I chuckled sarcastically.

"This is not something to laugh about. Your lack of respect for all that you do not understand will soon make itself an issue."

"Respect?" I said loudly, before Cyrus pulled me in closer to his body and shushed my loud mouth. Continuing in a whisper, I asked, "What sort of respect am I supposed to have? Bow down to her? Bow to her?" *Bow to the queen of slime.* The movie quote continued in my head uncontrollably as I waited for another cryptic response from my would-be suitor.

"You will remain calm," he hissed through clenched teeth. "There's a room full of people just beyond that wall that have no clue as to what is happening here. And they never should. You made the mistake of inviting yourself into her realm. It was you who did not accept her words graciously. It was you who used cursing words with her and left her in the wake of your anger. You caused this mess and there is no way I will allow you to cause a scene in the presence of nearly every Primus in the country. Do you know why Malcolm is the only Primus residing in the House of Porte?"

Shocked by his harsh words, I remained silent tucked tight against his chest as he hissed words into my ear with the faintest whisper. "Marienne trusts Malcolm with her House, obviously. If it were up to her, he would have been her Secondus. Do you think she would be happy to know you have angered such a strong local presence as Madam Azelie? I will tell you the answer to that obvious rhetorical question would be no. I have no time to school you on the happenings within our community. As of now, you know all that is important to you. There is someone, a very powerful someone, who clearly would like to see you suffer. Even if just a little bit."

My heart began to beat faster as fear built inside me. Cyrus's words echoed in my already unstable brain. Despite my ability to take things to the extreme, I felt I was quite a rational person and didn't believe for a second the woman actually had herself a set of fancy magical powers. I did, with all of my being, believe Cyrus thought she did. And that, in and of itself, was terrifying. If the person who you'd begun to view as a confidante, a protector should it come right down to it, was terrified of the scary lady, I might as well follow suit. Hell, he knew those idiots far better than I.

"Fine. Just take me back. If you won't allow me to go back to my seat, I want to go home. My home. I want to get on a flight tonight and go back home. This entire trip was a mistake." I shoved away from him and stomped off like a child. At least I wasn't covered in blood.

I stomped through the darkened hallway with such vigor I didn't see the obstruction in my path. My toe caught the edge of something immovable, and I stumbled over the top of it. In an effort to stay on my feet, my hands spread out in front of me and I caught myself on something partially pliable; squishy. Tucking my legs over the top of it, I flipped over onto my ass and turned to take a look at what had impeded my childish escape. In the murky darkness, I made out the shape of a body. Nude. A bit of wood protruded horrifically from between two modest breasts. A quick scream burst from my lungs and I scurried backward. I stared in horror. The woman's hands were bound with thick strands of colorless hair, muted by the darkness. The curiosity in me took over before I could stop it and I saw what I didn't want to see. Atop the shoulders, where a feminine head should be, a stump jutted upward instead. The jagged stump of what used to be a neck. The head lopped clean off.

Another yelp came from my throat, and I clamped a hand over my mouth. Heavy breaths spurted through my tightly clasped fingers.

"Dylan?" Cyrus said from his spot, standing a few feet from me, towering over the body that lay on the floor.

"Watch out," I said, holding out my hand as his feet shuffled through the body that lay on the floor. Like fog stuck to the ground, the body dispersed into the air with the motion of his feet across it.

"What? What is it?" He looked to me, his hands spread wide, reaching for my huddled frame.

"There," I said, pointing with shaking hands to the body that was no longer there. He looked around his feet at nothing. "It was right there."

"There's nothing here, Dylan. What did you see?" he asked as he knelt down to my level and grabbed hold of my arms. "What was it?" he asked through clenched teeth.

A light sob threatened to reveal itself, but I stifled it out of fear. Crazy was one thing. A big fat pussy was a whole other bucket of worms.

"A body," I whispered through jagged breaths.

Batshit crazy I is.

SIXTEEN

AS QUICKLY AS I COULD, I SCRAMBLED TO MY FEET. ON unsteady legs, I stood wobbling back toward the wall behind me.

"What?" Even in the dim light, I could see the lines on his face deepen.

He lifted his feet and stepped back and away from me through the body that wasn't there anymore. The mist had dissipated leaving nothing but the memory seared into my brain. His hands still spread wide in search of my body to grab hold of.

My knees wobbled and I was thankful there was a wall at my back to catch my fall. I knew what I'd seen. I knew I wasn't making shit up. It wasn't my style. Something was causing the hallucinations. Something magical? Doubted it. Something medicinal? Much more likely. Serious brain tumor? Good God, I hoped not.

"What is happening to me?" I asked through drawn breaths in a voice barely above a whisper.

My hands clung to a railing, which was reassuringly secured firmly into the wall, holding me up. My brain swam with the visual of another headless corpse. Granted, I'd seen the real deal up close and personal a few months back, but one didn't generally assume seeing corpses was going to be more than a one-time thing. Headless naked bitches, blood pouring from phantom wounds, macabre dreams and bloody children, and shiny caskets, it was all too much for one little journalist to handle. Even big heap bad-ass Dylan Hart could only handle so much before she was in desperate need of strong alcohol. Shit, antipsychotics might've be in order.

"I believe it's time to leave," his voice held determination; it almost masked his fear completely.

Without a word, I let him wrap his strong arm around my corseted waist and lead me through the barely lit hallway. I wasn't hurt, physically anyway; there was no reason I couldn't walk myself out. But his way was better for both of us. He obviously needed to play the dashing prince and I, for one of the only times in my life, allowed myself to be rescued.

I fought hard to not limp, or whimper, or in some way feign some form of illness as we emerged from the darkness into the brightly lit lobby area. It felt ridiculous to be escorted by a dashingly handsome man and not be walking upright on my own. My inner pride wanted me to pretend as if my personal situation was far worse outwardly to explain away the need to be practically carried out the door. Other than the fact that I was almost certain there'd be white coats waiting out front, straightjacket and fully loaded syringes in hand. Being nuts was no excuse to be frail.

Luckily, the only living souls to lay eyes on the two of us were the two door openers, or whatever they were called, that'd gracefully opened the two extravagant doors when we first arrived. By the time we reached those doors, my breathing was returning to normal and the sensation of sheer insanity was fading away. Anger filled the void it left behind.

There had to be some reason, other than being flat out fucked in the head, for me to be hallucinating so severely with no psychotropic enhancements. None consumed willingly anyhow.

A car, that was not the one we'd arrived in, pulled through the curved drive and stopped precariously in front of where the two of us stood. If we'd been standing an inch further from the steps, we might no longer have had all of our toes.

A menacing laugh filled the cooling night air and a set of chills shook my body down to my toes. From the darkness to our left, she emerged.

Oh, look it's my best friend in the whole wide world.

"Do you like my gift, *'cher*?"

In the soft light of the porch lamps, I saw a hideous grin begin to twist at the corners of her mouth. Her piercing blue eyes glared at me through a set of thickly caked lashes. I noticed, while shaking in my boots, her beautifully wicked face was missing its eyebrows. Maybe they were merely too blonde as happened with certain people, but there was nothing to be seen in that particular lighting. It added a creep factor that made me want to rush into the vehicle that had nearly crippled me.

"You are not welcome, Azelie. I wish you to leave us now."

Cyrus spoke as if those words alone would rid us of the petite dreadlocked problem. I doubted it.

"Pffft," she scoffed through her teeth unattractively. Apparently, she didn't think so either. "These words have little meaning, boy," her words hissed from her perfectly bowed lips. "Your lover must learn her place." Her tiny finger pointed at me with a crook to it, like a little cream-colored hook.

"Why?" I said defiantly.

"Why?" she huffed. "Why? Question yourself 'dis, why you kill, aye?" Her voice was soft. That terrified me more than her screeching ever could. Quiet bitches were the ones who secretly plotted your death.

I stumbled over my words in my quick rebuttal. I really had a reason, really I did. I was being threatened. They'd kidnapped Tatum. They'd been slaughtering the innocent. Alright, maybe not innocent, but they killed women nonetheless. They deserved it. Those little bastards deserved it and I'd do it again if it came right down to it. "They needed killing," I said with the iciest cold tone I could gather.

A shrill laugh pierced the otherwise silent landscape. "Vigilante? This why I take your heart. This why I give you visions of death all 'round you." Her hands moved as she talked, like they were telling the story her voice left out.

"A punishment?" It was my turn to be shrill. "You want to punish me? Bah! Who the fuck are you to put me on a mental time-out for killing two boys who would've killed me in their place if I hadn't had the balls to do it first? Whoever you think you are, whatever you think you can do, fuck off with it. I don't buy into bullshit." I turned from the tiny woman and opened the backdoor of the waiting car.

"Marienne will not be happy when she hears about this. Using your powers against the escort of the Secondus of the House of Cailleadh could cost you your place in the entertainment troupe," Cyrus intervened.

Ooh, burn, I thought as I rolled my eyes at his foolishness.

"Marienne is ignorant and won't sway. She come to me for supremacy oils and gris gris. Marienne House survives on my power. You and your whore mean nothing to her."

I saw Cyrus physically cringe when she said the word whore. It really didn't bother me. I had bigger Cajun fish to fry.

"Why do I mean something to *you*? What the fuck have I done to cause this?" I tried hard to hide the desperation in my voice.

I wanted it to end. I dreaded the thought that the woman was capable of actually controlling my thoughts, by whatever means, and causing horrific visions. Not to mention the possibility it would go on as long as she desired, terrified me. My logic clung to the fact that things such as magic were not of the natural world. On the other hand, it was beginning to appear as though I was out of the loop of what lay beneath the sparkling top layer of our society.

"Blood on your hands." Her body slithered as she dropped her head to look through her dreary lashes. "*My* blood on your hands," her words hissed through her teeth.

"What?" I couldn't believe what I'd just heard. I'd never had her blood anywhere near me. "Are you out of your mind? I've never touched you."

"My blood on your hands. Thick, and red, and drippin' from your body." Her eyes bore into my head, searching for something in there somewhere. Seeking out subconscious knowledge.

"Are we talking metaphorically here… or…?" I was totally

lost and had the feeling the tiny witch woman was growing more and more irritated with me by the minute. In a way I liked it, but then again, I thought her irritation could lead to a serious ass kicking on my end.

The woman spoke not a word and simply continued her stare. A flash of images penetrated my mind. My hands shoving a pool cue deep into the soft flesh of the overweight jolly Samoan vampy boy that bloody night in May. Flashes of random images of familiar faces and insignificant instances filled tiny voids between the important stuff. The things I was certain were the key points in the situation. Suddenly, I was watching myself tumble down the concrete steps, wrestling with the lanky Diego. We landed hard at the foot of the stairs and crashed into stacks of white five-gallon buckets. They cracked, tipped and spilt syrupy red blood in a gory mess. It covered the floor beneath us, splattering across my face, soaking my clothing, and seeping around the body of the poor vampire boy, who was unlucky enough to land on the bottom of the pile. Blood trickled and pooled along the concrete floor quickly, but I caught a glimpse of familiar symbols painted sporadically around the area.

Seeing it from another's eyes opened up so many new opportunities for a better camera angle. I watched my face contort with fear and so much rage until I almost didn't recognize myself. I watched as I lifted a piece of broken pool cue and jammed it into the sloppy wound left over from my bullet. Being a bystander, the scene horrified me. It was even more horrifying that the murderess was me. Granted, I was fully within my right as a human being to protect myself and the lives of others by any means necessary, but that didn't forgive the look that passed over my eyes right before I shoved that piece of wood, my makeshift stake, deep into the boy's broken flesh. I looked satisfied when it plunged into his chest.

My vision flashed white, as if someone took a photo too close to my face, and I was back in the present. Only, the scene was a bit different. I was sitting on the asphalted driveway, a few feet from our waiting car, staring up at Cyrus and his overtly concerned face. I shook my head and felt a little like a cartoon character shaking off a bad fall. Little yellow birds and stars twinkling overhead.

Azelie stood only a few feet from us. I wondered how long I'd been in psycho-land and why Cyrus allowed that crazy woman to get so close to us. More than that, for obvious reasons, I wondered what in the fuck had just happened to my already fragile mind.

"What…?" I asked in a voice that sounded nothing like my own. I sounded like a child waking from a nightmare. So tiny. So scared. Fuck that. "What in the fuck did you do to me you evil bitch?" Yelling from your spot on the ground was generally ineffective. In case you were wondering.

"It is what you've done, bitch." That word didn't fit the tiny girl. It seemed somehow beneath her.

"Ugh, I have no idea what you're talking about. Please, for the love of all that is Holy, tell me what I've done to you so we can move on with our lives."

Cyrus held his hand out and I took it. It was not the time to question chivalry. A flash of a memory, not of the actual event, but from the images that'd just popped into my head, symbols on the floor. Symbols I'd seen wrapping around the itty-bitty waist of my assailant.

How interesting.

I stood, feet firmly planted to the earth. Determination in my voice, I let the little bitch in on my theory. "What did you have to do with Diego and Sam and the lot of the dead hookers in California?" I saw Cyrus from the corner of my eye turn his head to face me so quickly I'd have thought it would spin right off his shoulders. Quite glad that didn't happen.

She chuckled softly and looked at Cyrus. Not me. "You stay, boy." Her little crooked finger came up and pointed at him, commanding him like a dog to stay put. The funny part was it apparently worked. She turned to me, finger still aimed at Cyrus. "You come here, my house, the Loa brought you. Loa brought you to punish. My vindication."

What the fuck is a Loa?

"It was you. I can't believe it. How? Why?" I stammered on flabbergasted at the outlandish situation. How in the world did I end up walking right into her shop? If I ever believed in fate, it was at that moment. "What in the fuck do you need gallons of dead hooker blood for?" I wasn't even yelling anymore. My shoulders slumped, I saddened at the situation. It was one thing when I thought they were only a couple of kids who lost their way in the seedy underworld of sex, blood, and rock 'n' roll. In that moment, knowing there was a purpose, a specific person controlling the operation, it felt too Jonestown for my maximum level of coping with life.

"What reason do I need? You have taken it from me and I want it back." Her petite shoulders lifted slightly and dropped with little effort. A shrug that said she cared not a lick about what she'd done. About the lives she'd cost.

"You're a fucking lunatic." My words blended together with frustration and out-and-out disbelief. "I should kill you where you stand."

Fucking TSA!

"Oh, but you have no sticks." She laughed at me. I hated

being laughed at.

My brows set low over my eyes, I tightened my jaw. "I don't need a fancy stick to kick your fucking teeth in." Spit sputtered through my teeth as I spoke through a set jaw.

Her laugh grew and echoed through the quiet night air until I couldn't take it anymore. Unhindered by my low-heeled boots, I took off in an all-out sprint toward that incessant laughter. Dress crinkling loudly around my legs, it only took a handful of long strides to reach the tiny woman. I leaped at her and landed square in the center of her body like a seasoned linebacker. She crumbled under my weight and I was glad, for the first time in my life, I was so damn big. We landed, one on top of the other, on the cold concrete walk that circled the driveway. Unlike every catfight you'd ever seen in your life, there was no hair pulling. She'd already gotten all the hair she needed from me. Without another thought, I reared my fist back and released it with all my fury into her dainty face. I heard a crack and knew I'd broken her nose. She wanted blood she could have a bit of her own. Her tiny hand came from nowhere and cracked me across the jaw sending my head spinning on my shoulders. She was stronger than she looked. Must've been all that hooker blood. I used both hands and wrapped them tightly through her thick dreads. Using them as leverage, I pulled her closer to my face so we were eye to eye. Sitting with all my weight on her legs, I had the advantage and was confident in my positioning. I was thankful for that. I was thankful for the littlest miracles as of late. I was thankful my tits stayed right where they should be.

"Why? Tell me why? How? How in the fuck did you orchestrate that massacre?"

She smiled with bright red blood trickling down her lips

from her cracked nose. "I see all. I am all. I want all."

"Power? That's it? Jesus, run for president for God's sake. What makes you think hooker blood will give you *all*?" I spat my words into her pretty little face while I clung to her tightly coiled hair.

"Specific, very specific offerin's." Her teeth were turning a lovely shade of red from her blood.

"Fuck you, cryptic bitch." I released one hand from her hair. Holding her tightly with the other hand, I reared back again and came down with a crack to her face. "I am so goddamned tired of you mother fuckers being so fucking cryptic!" I screamed into her face until I felt the tender skin in my throat scratch under the pressure. My fist came down on her bloody face again and again and again until her blood splashed across my face.

Hands wrapped around my waist and life became a series of slow motion events. Strong arms held me tight as they pulled my heavy body from atop the bloody mess of Madam Azelie. My hand let go and my body went a little limp. Tiny screams came from my bloody throat and I spat red from my mouth. I wanted to kill her. I wanted my strong fists to pummel her perfect face into the pavement. She was the reason I was in that mess. It was her. It was all her. It had always been her. Why? I had no fucking clue. How? Who the fuck knew. But I for damn sure wanted to know more. Mostly, I wanted to stop her. By any means necessary.

Cyrus cradled my body in his arms as he dragged my lifeless feet across the asphalt and toward the waiting car. The car, whose driver had never left his position at the wheel, was right where we'd left it in the driveway. My eyes never left the lifeless body of the bantam witch. She lay sprawled on the cold pavement, bleeding from her pretty little face, and I wanted to go back for more. My body didn't fight Cyrus; I knew in my subconscious, that I'd never win that fight. In my head, however, I was right back there with her, stomping her fucking murderous head into a pile of meat.

I watched her as Cyrus opened the car door and shoved me into it. He didn't bother pushing me across the seat before he crawled right over the top of me and took the seat behind the driver. My eyes stayed focused on the bloody heap on the ground a few feet ahead of the car. Cyrus mumbled something to the driver, it sounded French maybe, and the car began rolling forward. We were leaving. Driving away to safety and leaving that bloody mess behind. The car crept forward and moved past the body.

Air filled my lungs and stayed there. As we passed the bloody mess on the pavement, her little hand lifted. Wiggling tiny fingers, she waved at me, her white teeth flashed in a sardonic smile through a mask of blood.

I blinked my eyes hard, and when I opened them again, we'd passed her and were on our way out of the driveway and onto the main street. I twisted around and tried to look out the back window, but my attire didn't allow that much movement. In a last glimpse through a hurried glance out the back window, Azelie was gone.

I am fucked.

SEVENTEEN

MY BREATHS CAME IN RAGGED, HALF-CHOKED SPURTS. ALL the rage and homicidal urges had been ripped away the moment I watched that pretty, mangled face smile through all that blood I'd left behind. If she was strong enough to torment me after a beating like that, she was certainly strong enough to come back with a vengeance and beat the living shit out of me. If not worse. Hell, likely worse. She was, nevertheless, a murderess in her own right. Damn pot calling the kettle a murderous bitch.

"Eh, he, eh, she… she fucking smiled at me," I choked out in the general direction of Cyrus who was diligently checking every direction he could for further danger.

"You are an idiot, Dylan Hart." His words actually hurt my feelings. It was rare I allowed that to happen, but it did. My defenses were down, crusty exterior damaged, and raw core exposed.

"Well, fuck you too," I sputtered as I forced my corseted body to twist and turn to see in every direction. Fear made its way up the back of my throat and threatened to burst from my lips in the form of vomit. Or maybe it was the corset.

I leaned forward and looked out the front window in an attempt to calm my heaving stomach. I'd considered asking Cyrus to untie my laces, but thought against it. No bra and all. There were no traffic lights or traffic for that matter, and I knew we had to be close to home. Or the temporary home I'd left my shit in for the weekend. The headlights shined along the white line in the center of the road and I focused on that for a minute or two.

Fifty feet ahead, I picked up the silhouette of what looked like a dead animal in the road. If the driver didn't see it, we'd run it right over and spread the carnage even further. The car sped along and we grew closer to the image in our headlights. It was a body. It was a woman. Her naked chest evident in the bright lights of the car. The driver watched straight ahead—as hired drivers tended to do, your business was rarely theirs—seeming to not see the figure in the road. We barreled down the lane as I watched his foot never lift from the pedal. He was going to plow right into the woman in the street. Less than ten feet from the body, I saw the inevitable. Atop a lovely set of shoulders lay a bloody stump where a head should have been.

I thrust my body through the center of the bucket seats and screamed, "You're gonna hit her!" I pointed through the windshield directly at the headless body that lay flat along the darkened street. I was too late. The driver never had a chance to even try to stop. We plowed right through what should have been thick meaty flesh without even a thud. Fog spewed up over the hood and reflected the light from the headlamps.

Dead bitches popping up everywhere.

"Dylan!" Cyrus called from behind me, tugging at my dress.

"Miss, would you please take your seat. There is nothing in the road." The driver remained so calm I wondered if he was on drugs.

My body flopped back into my seat and I felt a sob on the fringes. "What's happening to me?" I asked in a voice barely above a whisper.

"Dylan, it's time to go home," Cyrus said without any precursor.

"What is happening?" I asked, feeling so weak, so suddenly, like someone had hit me with a tranquilizer dart. Not that I would know what that felt like.

"You are being cursed." His words hung thick in the air, I could reach out and touch them.

"That's not true," I argued, hardly able to open my eyes anymore. Tears were imminent. I felt them coming, and my body did everything it could to prevent that. Soon, the anger would come back and stay for good until the threat was gone. It's was a vicious cycle that had allowed me to live a mostly normal life, thus far.

"At this point, turning your back on her magic will do you no good."

"She killed those girls, Cyrus. It was her." A tear squeezed from my closed lids and ran down my cheek.

"I know." His hand touched my face and stealthily wiped the tear away.

"Why?" I asked.

"I don't know."

"What are you going to do about it?" Not me. Someone else

could handle it. I was officially clocking out.

"I'll inform Malcolm. But first, I am putting you on a plane back home. You are going to call Mike." I scoffed and rolled my head toward him. "You are going to call Mike, you will need him, and you are going to tell him to pick you up at LAX and take you to his house. You will wait there until we get back."

"Isn't going home enough? The bitch can't get me five hundred miles away." Seemed legit.

"Just do it. Until now, Dylan Hart has done whatever Dylan Hart has wanted to do and it has put you into a position you may not get out of unharmed. Now, you will do what I tell you to do and maybe you'll survive this mess. Until then, consider yourself cursed." His hand gripped my arm as his words spewed through clenched teeth.

"And who in the fuck are you? I don't see any shining armor lying around anywhere, so I doubt you're here to rescue me." My eyes were open. In flooded the anger. "I would've never gotten into this mess had it not been for that bitch in the first place. I wouldn't be here. I wouldn't know you. None of this shit would even exist to me if it weren't for her murderous greed. Malcolm, Dominika, you, all of this vampire bullshit would not even be a thought in my head without *her*. That bitch. Now, now, I'm seeing headless things lying about. I'm flailing around on the floor bleeding to death from phantom wounds." His eyes squinted. "Waking from dreams of bloody children and dying from your bite amongst shiny coffins in the basement." Cyrus clenched his jaw and shifted his brows, and I knew I'd struck a chord. "I'm right, aren't I?"

"You've been hallucinating." He waved his hand through the air as if waving away my words.

"But how much of that was surrounded by truth?" My boobs

heaved up and down with each eager breath that found its way past my lips.

Seconds passed with no response from Cyrus. The car quickly approached the macabre antebellum where we'd been staying. I stared at the man, clenched jaw, flared nostrils. He was hiding something, and I was going to find out what.

My hand was perched atop the handle of the door when the car rolled to a stop at the curb in front of the house. I didn't give Cyrus another second to react before I flung the door open and bolted up the walk. My heels clacked against the sidewalk. Stopping for a millisecond to open the iron gate, I ran as fast as my fat little legs could carry me. I ran up the walk, through the beautiful darkened landscape, and onto the shadowed porch. It'd never occurred to me that the door might've been locked when I started running, but feet from the door it dawned on me. Not risking the chance of looking back, I stuck my hand out and grabbed hold of the brass knob. It turned freely and I swung it wide open, rushing in ahead of Cyrus.

My feet slid across the slick floor as I tried to gain traction through the entryway and toward the door below the stairs. I'd left the door open, but I didn't care. In fact, it was the only light I had to show me the way. No one was home. They were all still back at the banquet hall enjoying their fancy dinner and camaraderie. I, on the other hand, was running through the empty, dark house of the Primus of the House of Porte, in search of a basement full of caskets likely there to house the undead. Or, the *supposedly* undead.

I slid to a stop and slammed into the adjoining wall next to the door under the stairs. It was obvious someone had gone overboard with the floor buffer. I had to see for myself. Before my weekend of an endless night closed up shop, I had to know if there were coffins in that basement. It really didn't do me any good in the end. It didn't change much. Only proved my dream was spot on. Or maybe it hadn't been a dream at all. Nothing changed unless it proved that all along, those harmless Sanguinarians had in fact been the real deal. Then, of course, that changed everything.

My shaking hand grasped the knob and turned it over in one smooth motion. Cyrus called from the walkway, still chasing after me. I had no time to wait around and see. I took the stairs two at a time not caring if I ate shit and tumbled head first down the stone steps. At least I'd be at the bottom. I bounded down, toward the dim candle light that waited at the end. It was exactly as I'd dreamt it. I knew, just knew when I reached the end, around that wall, there would be rows of shiny, lacquered coffins. If there were coffins, if it was exactly as I'd dreamt it, what was to say it was a dream at all? What was to say that was the reality and I had woken at seven in the morning, only to be placed back in my room by my vampire suitor. My head played the scene over and over as I approached the end of the line. The moment of truth was upon me as my foot hit the bottom floor.

I stumbled, but an arm wrapped itself around my waist and stopped me from tumbling forward to hands and knees. Before I could regain myself, the arm pulled me up and away from the bottom of the stairs. I leaned forward as far as I could trying to peer around the stone wall. At the edge of my vision, I caught a shimmer of shiny, lacquered wood gleaming in the candle light. I kicked my feet and fought against the arm that carried me away from my discovery and back up the steps into the house.

Faster than I'd made it down, I was back up and tossed onto the slick wood floor. I slid on my butt when I hit the floor with a thud. The front door was still open and allowed light to spill in and onto the face of Cyrus standing over me. He glared at me through his thick, fanned lashes. In his period garb, I felt like I'd been carried back in time to an era where men controlled their women by force.

"What in the fuck are you doing? What are you hiding?" I asked from my spot on the floor. It was the second time I'd yelled at someone from sitting on the ground and I was beginning to feel kind of stupid about it.

"What the fuck am *I* doing?" he asked in a huff and paced the floor in front of me. "Do you realize where you are? Do you have any clue what you're getting into? What you've already been involved in? You are so ignorant to the world you live in." He shook his head. "You're going to get yourself killed."

"What's in that basement? A coffin? There's a coffin down there. More than one." I was beginning to feel like Charlie Brewster.

"Do you not realize there are more pressing matters at hand here? Like the fact that there's a very pissed off high priestess after you right now." The fancy demeanor he liked to have in my presence disappeared and a jerky guy took its place.

"Stop skirting around the issue," I pressed.

"Ugh." He held his hands around his head. "Get up. Go get what you need. You have five minutes, or the car leaves you here with me. And her." He stopped moving, stopped breathing and stared at me until I thought he was going to crawl right inside. "Go. Now."

Going against everything that made me up as a human being, I got up. I got up and ran up the stairs as fast as I could. I never even looked back at him. No matter how much I wanted to know the truth. No matter how badly my curiosity wanted to know everything it could. I knew that curiosity didn't just kill cats. It also killed nosey little journalists who didn't know when to get the fuck out of town.

I counted on Cyrus to make some kind of travel arrangements for me while I got my shit. Either that or he was going to let me sit alone at the airport and wait on standby until something opened up. I honestly didn't care either way. I just wanted out. I wanted to go home.

I pulled my phone from my clutch purse and plopped on the edge of the bed. I really didn't want to call Mike. In fact, he was the last person I wanted to know about my predicament, but Cyrus was right, to an extent. Mike needed to be aware of the situation. He was hard at work on the headless chick case, and the fucking perpetrator fell right into my lap. No matter how hard it was to believe. Sometimes truth really was stranger than fiction.

With an over-the-top sigh, I dialed Mike. The line rang on and on while I rehearsed what I'd say in my head. I'd tell him I was in trouble and he'd get melodramatic and blame it all on me. I'd tell him how it wasn't my fault and he couldn't keep me locked up in a bubble. He'd tell me how incorrigible I was and remind me he'd told me it'd end badly. I'd tell him to get fucked and he'd do just that. Nothing would be resolved, and I'd end up right back where I was, sitting in that room all alone, only I'd be pissed off at one more person. Another sigh and his voice mail picked up. I listened to his spiel and left my condensed message after the tone. He hadn't answered. No matter how much my outward bad-ass protested his assistance, on the inside, I knew he was the only one I could really count on. Sometimes I wished I would've realized that sooner, or at least admitted to it. We had too many issues to ever be a thing again, but a piece of me missed him fiercely and wished I could take back all I'd done.

I shook my head and rid myself of those thoughts. Living in the past would get you nowhere but ass backwards, so I just didn't do it. Leaving thoughts of Mike for a more appropriate venue, I stood and began the ridiculous dance of trying to remove my corset.

Buttons lined the front from the bust to my waist, it was how I'd put it on originally, but since Tatum had tightened my cinch, it'd become nearly impossible to get enough leeway on a button to undo them. I tried to reach behind my back and tug at the string to loosen the lacings, but I couldn't even find the ends of the knot. One hand reached over my shoulder and the other up from the curve of my back, an attempt to come at it from both ends, but my fingers never found the looping tendrils of a silky bow. Grunts and groans escaped my throat as sweat began to bead around my hairline. I spun like a dog chasing its tail and knew I probably looked like a fucking idiot dancing around just trying to get undressed. How idiotic it all was, vampires and witches and corsets, oh my!

"Son of a cock sucking whore. Where the fuck is it?" I yelled into the stale air that filled my lonely room.

I jumped at the sensation of a soft touch between my shoulder blades. "Let me get that," a much calmer Cyrus spoke from behind me. He'd snuck in the door during my groaning.

I let him help me out of sheer frustration, but honestly did not want him touching me. Really. A slight popping sound and instant relief. I'd never felt something so divine. A corset coming undone was better than sex. The fact that my boobs were in their natural habitat again was so freeing I craved more. I wanted my sweats and oversized socks to go with the hanging titties. I let out a heavy sigh of relief and remembered I wasn't alone. Instinctively, I grabbed my chest, folding both arms across. My corset slid down my waist and over my hips leaving my top half-naked.

I felt Cyrus's stare on my bare back and wanted nothing more than to put a shirt on. "Uh, thanks. I thought I'd never get that fucking thing off." A nervous chuckle spewed out and I kept my back to him.

"You're welcome." His voice sounded funny, like he'd been running and was out of breath. "I… I'm sorry." His hand laid flat in the center of my back and stayed there. The heat emanating from his palm was oddly calming.

I bet he gives killer massages.

Shut up, inner–Dylan. You don't know what you're talking about.

"Well, yeah, I'd like to get dressed." I dropped my head a bit and listened for his footsteps. After a few moments of silence, he turned from me and headed out the way he came in. "Hey," I called to him. Turning only partially, to meet his eyes, I asked, "Do I have a way home tonight?"

Cyrus dropped his eyes to the floor when he saw I was half-turned in his direction. "Yes, I've made a call. There is no time to check your luggage. I'm sorry. Can you bring only your carry on and I will make sure your other bags are brought to you tomorrow?"

I hated to leave anything behind, but I'd rather my left belongings were clothes and shoes and not my Godforsaken head. I nodded gently in his direction to let him know I understood and turned away from him again. "Can you explain everything to Tatum for me?" If she gave two shits.

"Of course. I'll wait for you in the foyer." He shut the door gingerly as he left me alone in my room.

I stood quietly, half-naked and alone in my room. My eyes

caught a glimpse of the mirror that should've been a window. I couldn't pack my shit fast enough. Grabbing only the essentials, I shoved a straightener, makeup bag, shampoo, and as many clothes as I could fit in the shoulder bag I'd brought as a carry-on. I hadn't even put my shirt on yet. Boobies flying everywhere, I tossed my important shit in my bag and packed my suitcase with the rest. I didn't want to rely on anyone else to take care of that. Strapping into a bra, I stripped the rest of my getup off and threw on my yoga pants and Optimus Prime t-shirt, pulled on my Converse, and called it a day. Voodoo bitches, fucked up vampire basement shit, crazy Cyrus, I'd had enough. I was done.

Halfway out the door, something made me turn around. I didn't know what you'd call it, intuition maybe. There was something in my head that I should've listened to far more often, and that time I did. I pulled my phone from my bag and went back into the trashed room for one last thing. The camera on my phone wasn't the best, but I used the video camera to capture the frame of the mirror. I'd never be able to describe it properly, and I didn't want to forget that image. Someone, at some point, when all the mystical crap blew over, would be able to tell me what the hell it was.

My soft-soled shoes made no noise as I tromped along the carpeted third floor. It felt wrong to leave my things behind and the room a disaster. Oh hell, fuck the room. I didn't want to lose out on a quarter of my wardrobe running away from my problems. Granted, those problems caused seriously gory hallucinations and threatened my life; there was no shame in running away from imminent danger.

I trotted down the first staircase and along the second-floor landing. I could see Cyrus over the edge of the railing waiting patiently at the foot of the last staircase. He'd lost the hat and coat, but still wore a snazzy pair of black suspenders and starched white shirt. He'd turned lights on in the foyer, and both front doors were open wide. I wondered if he'd ever shut them to begin with or if he was just that anxious to get rid of me.

I was at the top of the stairs when I caught her image in the open doorway. Dried blood caked her creamy skin, but she seemed undeterred by the injuries she'd sustained at my hand. At first, I thought she was a vision, a nightmare while I was awake like the headless girls. I blinked my eyes tight and opened them to find Madam Azelie still standing in the doorway. I tried to shake off the vision, praying she would just poof into smoke like the others. Nothing changed. The tiny woman stood in the doorway and stared at Cyrus. No one spoke, and I wondered if Cyrus saw her too. I thought for a second about throwing something at her to see if she dissipated like the others, but decided against it. My luck I'd miss and break something or hit my target and piss her off even more.

As I watched the scene unfold below, I noticed Cyrus wasn't moving. Not at all. Most humans moved eventually, even just a little. It was nearly impossible to hold completely still for any length of time. Try it sometime. She hadn't seen me yet, she was too focused on the vampire boy a few feet from her. I wished I knew where things were located in the massive house. Like a back entrance for example. I wished I had a plan, even a half-cocked plan, at that point. I wished I had my gun.

I looked around, frantically trying to find anything to inspire some amazing feat of heroism. The second floor held nothing but a tiny wooden table with a lovely vase and flowers on it. Not exactly what I had in mind. Another check on Cyrus let me know he was stuck in the world's longest staring contest but apparently unscathed. For the time being.

As quietly as I absolutely could, I crept along the landing, past the head of the stairs, and into the hallway I'd yet to step foot in. I was hidden from view but had to figure something out fast because my gut told me the freak show downstairs was just about to come to a head and explode all over the slick wooden floor. Not a literal Scanners head explosion. Hopefully. Something had to give.

The hall was short, only three doors in all and nothing but a few miscellaneous paintings along the walls. Hoping everyone was away at the ball, I tried the knobs. Knob number one, locked up tight. Knob number two clicked over and swung freely to the wall. I flipped the switch, and vanity lighting illuminated a maroon bathroom complete with a claw foot tub. I shut the door behind me and searched each drawer and cabinet for some kind of weapon should it come to that. I knew it would. It always came to *that*. I tried so hard to be quiet, but the longer it took to drudge up a plan, the more frantic I became. The longer it took me to figure out how I'd get out of the house, the more I yearned to go home. I wanted nothing more than to leave the vampire malarkey and that crazy bitch behind me. At least, until she infiltrated my dreams again.

"Fuck," I groaned with my hands on my hips, frustrated at the lack of deadly weapons the bathroom held.

Moving onto the third knob, I listened for any tell that the situation had changed downstairs. Nothing. Not one sound. Something was amiss on the first floor of the House of Porte, and I for one did not give one furry turd what it was. Unless, of course, it changed my current situation of being alive. The knob was stuck tight. Apparently, vampire folk weren't all that trusting of others.

"Shit, shit, shit," I whispered through a hurried breath.

My hands flew up to my head and held there; fingers laced together, cradling it in frustration. My heart thumped faster at the thought of having to confront evil incarnate. I closed my eyes and let my hands fall to my knees as I bent at the waist. Breathing through the fear, my thoughts ran rampant through my head. There was no other choice but to go down those stairs. No windows to escape through. No service entrance. No heavy armory in the bathroom drawers.

I pulled air into my lungs and shoved it out over and over again psyching myself up. I stood and bounced on my toes like a boxer before a fight. The overly packed bag I had slung over my shoulder bounced with me. The feel of the weight on one shoulder reminded me of the night I'd worn it to Midnights Dream. The night that would go down in infamy as the night I killed two boys and started a war between a New Orleans voodoo priestess and Dylan Hart. The night it cradled my gun gently within its canvas shell. Unfortunately for me, it was not serving that particular purpose anymore. Maybe it was lucky. My lucky bag. I'd never thought of it as a lucky bag before, but that night it had the chance to prove itself worthy of that title.

Limbered up and as ready as I'd ever be, I tiptoed toward the head of the stairs. Sticking to the wall nearest the stairs, I slid my body along the expensive wallpaper toward my target. At the corner, I stopped and calmed myself.

In a moment, I told myself, *you're going to come face to face with a tiny girl who wants to take your head clean off your shoulders. It'd be best not to let that happen.* I gave myself an encouraging nod and poked my head around the corner to check the situation.

Blood caked buttery skin met me in the middle, close enough

to kiss. Instinctively, my body flung backward away from the threat. Thick dreads surrounded the petite frame and hung nearly past her ass in thickly matted strips. I was still on my feet but got the distinct impression that wouldn't last long. At some point, the woman had ditched Cyrus and moved on to find her true prize. Me.

Cyrus was somewhere in the house, maybe dead, I didn't know, but he wasn't sneaking up behind her with a heavy object to bonk her on the head with, so it really didn't matter where he was. I was, for obvious reasons, more concerned with keeping my frizzy head planted firmly on its shoulders.

The tiny woman moved closer to me, backing me further and further against the wall at my back. Soon I'd be left with nowhere to go and nothing to do but succumb to the inevitable.

"What do you want from me?" my voice came out shaky and scared. Not a good sign.

"You? Penance."

Oh, that's all?

"I'm sorry I ruined your blood collection, but I was trying to stay alive, you have to respect that, right?" I chuckled trying to keep the moment light. Yeah, right.

"Nothing for you but to suffer."

"So, you're not planning on lopping my head off?" I asked, hoping the surprise I felt was warranted.

"You, my darlin', will pay penance for your actions. Not die, live… cursed." Her bloody face gave no hint as to her true intentions.

That didn't sound too bad. Better than dying, I figured. "Don't you have to believe in that shit for it to have an effect? I don't *believe* so have at it with the cursing." Childishly, I folded my arms across my chest and planted my foot to one side. Bitch stance, executed.

"Aye, you believe, you believe 'cause you must. 'Cause you seek truth."

"Fuck me. For God's sake can you people please stop speaking in riddles? It's not fun, it's not fancy, it's annoying, and I'd like you to stop, please." I changed my mind; I didn't care if she took my head off.

"Listen, child, 'dis what you need know." Her frail body slithered toward me, but I had nowhere left to go. The little bitch had backed me into a corner. Literally. "By heart, put 'dis to work." Her hand lifted, rosary still wrapped firmly around it, and she blew a puff of dust into my face with force. "By soul, take 'dis mind." She swiped her hand across my face and smeared it with oily goo leaving it slick and filthy.

"What the fuck are you doing to me?" I might've been smashed, chin tucked to my chest, and my back against a wall, but that didn't mean I wanted shit smeared all over my face. Using both hands, all my force and the biggest set of balls I could muster, I shoved the little woman away from me. Her small body stumbled backward and slammed into the floor. With the back of my hand, I wiped at the crap she'd smeared down my face. "Go fuck yourself," I hissed down at her delicate frame sitting upright on the carpeted floor.

Laughter built in her throat and spilled from her lips, tickling the hairs on my neck, and causing them to stand on end. "I believe you are the one who's *fucked*." She cackled and giggled as she rose from the floor. Her crooked finger came up and pointed to the center of my chest. She started speaking again, much deeper and in a language I didn't understand. Her lips moved quickly, quicker than the words that spewed from her mouth. It looked like a horribly dubbed foreign film. But scary.

Really, pretty fucking scary.

A tingling started between my boobs and spread slowly outward. After a few moments, it didn't tingle so much as burn. No, blister. Scorch. Fucking hurt like hell. A guttural scream came from somewhere in me, and I bent over in pain. The tiny finger pointing at me, the odd voice coming from the little terror, nothing compared to the fear I felt as my heartbeat stopped.

I coughed and sputtered, and tried to will it to start again, but nothing helped. Seconds felt like hours the moment I felt my source of life cease to function. My knees collapsed and my heavy body hit the floor with a thud. Mouth gaped open, I sucked in air like a fish out of water. A guppy to be exact. Suffering was not a strong enough word to describe what the little bitch was doing to me. She wanted penance, retribution for my actions, and she was taking her pound of flesh straight through my chest cavity.

I riled, writhed, died on the floor at her feet but her power never wavered. Fiction or fact, it didn't matter anymore, I believed. Against everything I'd ever known, felt, learned, in that moment, I knew things existed that shouldn't. Things most people would rather stay hidden behind the veil of falsity. Curses had power, whether you believed it or not. I didn't, and look where it got me.

My vision hazed at the edges. A fancy white vignette surrounded my view. A kinked smile twitched at the ends of Azelie's mouth. A disdainful scoff followed and she dropped her finger. "Now, you believe."

My heart fluttered back to life and I gulped in air faster than my lungs would allow. Each felt as if it would burst under the pressure. Tears flowed down my cheeks without my control. I hated crying, but dying was far, far worse.

"Why?" my pathetic half-dead voice choked out.

"You're a nosy little thing. A good ally." She squatted next to me coming almost to my level. "You, my darlin', will be mine." Her smile spread wide across her face.

"No, why *them*?" I asked, starting to come around again, but still not really making sense with my line of questioning.

"Your mind makes up the visions. I only make sure they yours to see." That explained the horrific things I'd been seeing, sort of, but it wasn't what I was after.

"No." I shook my head, hoping she'd get the hint and tell me something before torturing me further. If I was going to die, I at least wanted to go out feeling some sort of satisfaction.

The cat came back.

Her face scrunched. "My blood?" I nodded. "Blonde, all I need is blonde. Very specific sacrifice. No blood on my hands, no, no, no. Police come with white goat, no, no." She ticked her finger side to side and shook her head. "One sacrifice will do, but without the *lamb*, I need more life. More blood." She softened her face and spoke to me like I was her pupil. "Blood makes the magic stick. Gives it life. Blood is life."

It's always blood. Blood is life.

"Why California?" My voice was hoarse and hurt a little coming out.

"Easy. Very easy." She laughed a hearty belly laugh. "Vampires. Oh, blame the vampires. Stupid Americans believe anything. That's why I choose vampires, easy scapegoat. And easy zombie. Very… vulnerable. The young ones."

"You're pretty open about it all now. Figure you'll kill me anyway so why the hell not spill the beans?" I smiled, but it meant nothing. I only just wanted to get an idea of how long

I had.

"Oh, no, penance, *'cher*. You owe retribution."

"You keep saying that. Why aren't you just exacting your pound of flesh?"

"I don't want your blood. Ha, brunette." She lifted a lock of my hair. "I want *you*." Her dainty hooked finger poked me in my chest. "Your soul is in my pocket. Your thoughts are mine. I have what I need to replenish what you stole from me." She lowered herself and tilted her head to meet my eyes. "I have you."

My heart, though still beating, flipped and fluttered with her words. "Who took their heads?" I asked as I gulped down the fear that crept up my throat.

"Others. All the others. One at a time." She explained as if I should already know. "'Dis America, *'cher*. You can't have bodies layin' around. And witnesses are easier handled when they dead."

"And the hair?" Nothing made sense, but it all made perfect sense.

It's magic, silly girl. Why else?

"Binds the spirits. Angry souls are not good." She smiled again as if it was a wonderful sunny day in the park.

"And the heads? What purpose does that serve?" I wanted everything. All the bullshit behind the bloody mask. The more I kept her talking, the longer I had to devise a plan. Or, at least that's how they did it on TV.

"Vampires, *'cher*. You should know, you've taken a few heads yourself." She looked me in the face like I was the dumbest little puppy she'd laid eyes on.

Oh, that.

"Yes, but they're—" I argued.

"There's no difference. Make no excuses." Anger rolled off her.

"No, I meant they're not really vampires. Just killing them like normal people will work." Probably.

"So innocent." She patted the top of my head and rose from her place next to my head.

"I just want to go home." I played to her softer side. If one existed. "Can I please just go home?"

"You can go wherever you'd like." I sighed, but she continued. "Where ever you run, I be there." She stood over the top of me, staring down like I was a bug at her feet. "I am your thoughts. I am your soul."

I swallowed hard and fought against the fear that built inside me. All wanted was to go home. I wanted to be away from that place. Away from her and Malcolm and Cyrus and the lot of them. The girl leaned over the top of me holding some kind of piece of coal. A flick of her wrist and the charcoal marked my skin, creating symbols along my arm.

A burst of adrenaline rushed through my veins and forced my tired muscles to function. I grabbed her wrist with my free hand and held her in place while I lifted my legs and kicked her hard with both feet. The soles of my shoes landed square in her core, and she flew backward. Her rosary left dangling from my fingers. She might have had magical powers and shit, but the bitch was still human. I could kill a human. Apparently I could also kill vampires.

As Azelie tumbled to her ass, I shoved mine up off the floor and climbed to my feet. I didn't waste a glance back at her. My short legs scurried across the carpeted floor and down the stairs with a bound. Cyrus still stood in his position at the foot of the staircase, motionless as a statue.

"Cyrus!" I called to him. He didn't turn toward my voice.

My feet hit the slick wood floor, but the rubber of my Converse prohibited the skid I'd grown accustomed to. I spun around the banister to meet Cyrus's eyes. They were blank, blanched nearly white, and dead.

"Cyrus?" I screamed in his face. Not a movement.

I raised my hand and landed a slap across his cheek. Nothing. His droopy eyelids didn't even blink under the sting of my blow.

"Ugh," I groaned in frustration. "I don't have time for this shit."

My feet took off with a jolt and carried me out the front door and down the walk. At the end of the walkway, parked in the street where we'd left it, the shiny black car waited for me. I sent a little prayer up to the Big Guy for a miracle and barreled down the path toward the waiting car. Along the concrete walkway, squiggly white lines lead the way toward the car.

Without stopping completely, I slowed enough to catch a better view of the new artwork adorning the pavement. Crudely drawn snakes wiggled in white chalk designs underfoot. My soft soled shoes slapped the pavement, smudging the chalk drawings with every step. I heard cackling laughter behind me as I opened the rear door.

"Run away, child," Azelie called from the open doorway at the other end of the walk. "I wit'chu always." Her thick accent echoed through the night, sending prickling chills from my neck down the backs of my legs.

"Go fuck yourself!" I yelled back just before I slammed the car door shut. "Drive," I told the man behind the wheel.

Azelie's laughter filled the cab of the car even as we pulled away from the curb and headed off into the darkness.

"Where to?" the driver spoke finally.

"Home. I just want to go home," I said, leaning my head back onto the headrest.

I licked my fingers and rubbed vigorously at the black she'd left on my arm. It smudged but didn't disappear. I tried the same with the oily shit on my face. Using the rearview mirror, I could see there was nothing obvious spread across my face, but it was still oily to the touch.

"Fuck it," I whispered to myself and slid back into my seat.

The single person, who was responsible for the deaths of over fifteen women, had become my arch nemesis. I could've pinned Diego and Sam on her. In a roundabout way, it was her fault. It was her fault I killed people. It was all her fault. All because she didn't want to get her hands dirty sacrificing one herself? Not saying that was any better, but come on, do your own dirty work.

And for what? Power? Greed? Somehow, that wicked voodoo bitch had orchestrated the serial murders of women in California, Nevada, Texas, and who knew which other states. Only girls were beheaded, bound and left for the vultures. Were there other Sams? Other Diegos? Other stupid kids with nothing better to do than follow blindly? How did she find any of them? So many questions filled my always curious mind. One time, just one time, my curiosity needed to save my life instead of digging me deeper into shit.

My fingers twisted the beads of the black rosary as I rested my head and my tired eyes. I'd slept so long, yet felt so tired as if I hadn't slept at all. It'd been two days since I'd seen the sun. An endless night of horrors and blood that seemed to stretch beyond my memory. Hours left until dawn, I yearned for the light of day. Away from the monsters, away from the witches, the ghosts, the vampires, I clung to the only thing I had in my possession. Faith. Faith in myself and my steely friend at home on the nightstand.

If it's real, all of it, someone has some serious explaining to do.

EIGHTEEN

MY PLANE LANDED AT QUARTER-TO-FOUR AT THE ALWAYS crowded LAX. The lights of the city sparkled wildly. A lovely homecoming, but bittersweet. I gotten a red eye flight back home after a terrifying encounter with a hell bitch. With no friendly distraction, I'd spent my flight white knuckling it with visions of fiery crashes and mile long plummets from space. All the while, the fear of darkness loomed over me. Everything in my rationale told me it was idiotic; things like magic and vampires were fiction and nothing more. My heart still felt the sting of that woman's grasp and respected the existence of things otherworldly. My soul quivered in its skin sack for fear of contamination from that of greed-filled magic.

I felt at any moment I would teeter right off the deep end directly into insanity. And if I wasn't careful, I'd get locked up with the others. The others who said things that should not exist in our modern world were lurking in the shadows around them. Waiting for their turn to strike.

I thought I'd feel a sense of relief when I disembarked the aircraft. Relieved for the fact that my feet were planted firmly on the earth and I was no longer hurtling through open space at five-hundred miles an hour. That never happened. The sensation of being in air, seemingly free of curses and voodoo mamas, had created a false sense of security. Well, secure from the likes of witches and vampires anyhow. Once out of the terminal and on my way to hailing a cab, it truly sank in that I was all alone. No one in town would believe it if I told them I'd been cursed in New Orleans. Not even Mike. Especially not Mike.

I was pissed at Tatum for not being more aware of my predicament. Malcolm could go fuck himself for all I cared, but that was nothing new. Cyrus weighed heavily on my mind. I'd left him alone in that house with that woman. Under her spell. White-eyed and dead. A zombie. A fucking voodoo zombie. I clutched Azelie's black rosary in my hand and prayed to anything that would listen that my friend would make it out alive.

I dug my phone from my bag and dialed Tatum. She was my only link to the situation I'd left in my wake and, as far as I knew, completely unaware of any danger. Her line rang incessantly in my ear. Even her fucking phone suffered under the weight of that ginger fuck. Her voice mail answered and beeped, letting me know it was time to talk.

"Tatum, shit has hit the fan. I can't explain everything right now. If you're away from the house, go back right now. Cyrus is there and he's in trouble. I ran away and took a plane home." I paused for a long time, trying to figure out how to say what needed to be said. "Tatum, the person who killed those girls, the one who took Reggie's head, she knows who I am. She wants me dead. She has Cyrus and I don't know if he's okay or not." My voice shook with tears that clung to the edge of my lashes. "I need Malcolm to stop her from hurting anyone else until I can figure out how to fix this. I'm heading home now and I'm going to call Mike again. He needs to know." I took a deep breath, "Tatum, if I don't see you… I love you. Whatever happens, I love you. And thank you for pushing Cyrus. He's a really good person, regardless. Call me as soon as you can, please." Snot mingled with tears at the tip of my nose, and I decided to hang up before shit got out of hand.

Wiping tears away from my oily face, I stomped through the bulk of LAX. in search of an exit. At four a.m., the cabbies were all lined up along the walk waiting for the first all-nighter to hop in their yellow cesspool of phlegm and old urine. I didn't care. I just wanted to be in my own house so I could be crazy in private.

I'd packed in such a hurry I had nothing with me aside from what fit in my canvas bag. It didn't take much to slide into a stinking seat and mumble to the driver my destination. I hoped Tatum brought the rest of my shit with her when she came home in twelve hours. If she came. I could have run to the police. Fuck, I could have had the driver take me back to find Tatum and Malcolm. But I didn't. I didn't care about anything or anyone but myself. In a time of sheer fear, it was perfectly acceptable. I'd made an enemy in that town and I needed out and fast. There was rarely a better option than leaving the direct turf of said enemy in times of war. I was pretty good at making enemies. A talent I had.

The driver spoke nearly no English which worked for me, I wasn't really into talking. Azelie's black rosary, dangling from my fingers, clicked against the armrest in the door. Mike hadn't called me back. He had no clue I was home, or in trouble, or in need of his assistance. I was home, yes, but I was so much more alone than I had ever been. In a way, being home by myself caused more fear than the aspect of coming face to face with that badass voodoo mama again.

I closed my eyes, but it only took a few seconds before visions of dead girls danced in my head. I opened my eyes and watched the scenery pass me by. Bright lights made way for suburbs and I knew I was close to home. We turned onto a side street and there were only a few blocks left until home. A heavy sigh pushed from my lungs and I let my head fall back again. Something pulsated in my peripheral, and my head turned into that direction instinctively.

Sitting upright in the seat next to me, as if it were the most normal thing in the world, a headless and naked body sat next to me. A squeal popped out of my mouth and my body flung itself backward as far as it could away from the corpse.

"No drunk in cab!" the driver yelled from the front seat in broken English. A woman screamed in his backseat and he assumed she's was drunk. Must've been Hollywood.

A large bit of wood protruded from between two naked breasts. Hands bound with black hair lay still in her lap. My breaths came heavier and heavier over the few seconds that passed. My eyes told me the stake in her chest was moving, but my brain wouldn't believe it. Up and down, in and out, as if moving with sets of breaths. I stared at the chest, trying to make out what I was seeing. My eyes trained on the woman's chest missed the movement coming from lower. Hands flung up into my vision and reached out for me. Fingers tense and wriggling around bands of knotted black hair.

I screamed. I screamed and flailed and screamed some more. My hands slapped through the hands that reached out for me. The hands and arms dissipated into smoke only to reform a second later. The car slammed to a stop, and my body flew forward with the momentum. My head slammed into the back of the passenger seat and knocked me senseless for a minute.

"Get out. No drunks in cab. Out of my cab. Out!" the driver yelled irrationally from his position behind the wheel.

The body had disappeared completely, for which I was thankful, but I was still a few blocks from home and now without a ride. My eyes sat wide on my shocked face. Unlike my normal self, I exited the vehicle without saying a word.

My ass slid from the seat, legs shaking when my feet hit the ground. I slammed the door shut with gumption just seconds before the cabby sped off. He didn't even wait for his money. Apparently, I'd scared the big tough Los Angeles taxi driver. At least I wasn't the only one that wanted to get the hell away from me.

Still shaken, I took off on foot toward home. The neighborhood was dark at that ungodly hour just before dawn leaving me alone in my own thoughts. I clung to my stolen rosary and prayed I'd make it home without another visit from my headless friends. If there were eight dead girls, my mind would show me eight. Right?

Fuck that. Fuck that. No. No. No! I am not doing it! Listen here mind, you stop it! Now! No more dead bitches!

My feet hit the pavement with light slaps, and it was the only noise that filled my ears. I passed an alley to my left and tried hard to not let my eyes wander in that direction. I tried not to let myself think about blue dumpsters and headless broads.

A growl rumbled through the darkness coming from

nowhere in particular. I stopped in my tracks and searched my surroundings for a rabid dog showing teeth from some darkened corner. Nothing came running for me. No glowing eyes shined in the streetlamp. I dug in my bag for my keys. I saw on T.V. once you should have your keys out and ready for use when walking alone at night. I shoved half of the keys in my back pocket, leaving a few dangling over my butt cheek for easier grabbing, just in case.

I forced my feet to pick up the pace as I headed for home. Through the sound of my rubber-soled shoes slapping the cement, another growl rang in my ears. I didn't bother to stop and look. Faster, I moved through the dimly lit street and around the corner at the end.

Louder the growls came until I heard them snarling and snorting in my ear and I swore there was a beast following close behind me. Without hesitation, my legs lifted nearly to my chest as I tore off in an all-out run.

Pounding paws hit the cement behind me. No matter how fast I pushed myself to run, the galloping beast stayed close behind. Snarling, snorting, jaws snapping their razor sharp teeth right at my neck. Or so my brain told me from the sound it emitted. My legs burned from the exertion of energy I was forcing upon them trying to escape whatever was following me.

Another corner, then one more and I'm home. Run, fat ass! Run!

Unearthly, animalistic noises tickled along my skin as the unseen beast growled its terrible growl. And gnashed its terrible teeth. I ran as fast as my fat ass could carry me. I ran until my lungs refused to fill with air. Ran and ran, until I thought I'd just fall down and wait for death to come. My hand clenched around the beaded rosary that hung through my fingers, and I prayed for help.

Mike's voice played through my head as my feet pounded the broken sidewalk toward home.

"When you run, I'll be there."

How true had that become? As my feet slapped the pavement, only a block from home, my phone rang somewhere deep in my bag. Images of dead things flashed through my head, and I tried my damnedest to keep them at bay, if only to keep from running into things in my path. I dug in my bag, frantically searching for my ringing phone. Beastly growls followed close at my heels as I ran. Fat girls didn't run, not unless being chased. And though my eyes didn't see the beast, my heart felt its presence, and my soul told me to escape that evil at all costs. My fingers found the slick plastic of my phone and brought it to my ear, answering it on the way.

"Mike," I cried into the receiver. "Help!" A scream escaped my heavy lungs, and the muscles in my legs burned as I picked up the pace to clear the last few hundred feet to the stairs of my apartment. I hadn't had time or energy for more. He'd called when I needed him, and I hoped he'd gotten the hint that I needed him so desperately. Knowing him, he was already on his way. I clutched the phone in my hand but didn't speak. Didn't even hold that damn thing to my face. I held onto it like a lifeline, just in case. Just in case, shit went down. If I died, I didn't want to be alone.

My breaths hardly came anymore. I just ran. Ran in the direction of home. Away from the growling, heavy footed thing at my back. Whatever it was that followed me from the cab, I had an idea who'd sent it after me. It was no dog. No natural animal chasing me home. Real or mystical, I hadn't the chance to find out, and I hoped I'd never have to. The thought of something unknown breathing down my neck terrified me. Send a wolf. A bear, a fucking Yeti, but like hell you shouldn't send some demonic beast to tail me home. Three legs, snarling unearthly jaws snapping at my flesh, devilish fur, talons to tear at guts, my mind ran rampant with wild images of possibilities.

Only feet away, I pushed my body to continue. It'd be a shame to lose after such a glorious escape. I ran as fast as my legs would allow. My left leg rose, subconsciously preparing for the first step of the stairs, only inches away. I lunged my body forward and my foot caught the step perfectly, landing flush with the old wooden step. In a heartbeat, my other foot caught up and carried me up another step.

The weight of death brushed at my heels. My muscles burned as I scrambled up the stairs. Out of pure instinct, I ducked just in time to clear the tree limb of death, but lost my balance and landed on the palms of my hands against the step. They stung with the pain of scraped skin, but I shoved on. Without a thought, my hands moved in unison with my feet and I scurried up the steps. I moved quickly, utilizing all four limbs. I reached the door and grabbed the keys dangling partially from my back pocket. I begged the universe to, just once, let my damn door open. I jammed the key in its slot and turned my quivering hand over. Breath escaped my lungs in a quick yip of joy when I heard the pins shift and felt the key turn over. With all my might, I shoved my body against the door as I turned the knob. For the first time ever, it flung open without instance. I felt dark evil looming over my back. It tickled my soul with its heartless feelers.

"No!" I screamed.

Not today, Satan.

I flung my hefty body into the darkened space that was my

apartment. As I did, I turned to face the open doorway and caught a glimpse of the beast at my heels. I fell firmly on my ass. As I stared out to the blackened porch, I saw nothing. Before me was an empty void, where what I'd imagined to be a huge hideous drooling monstrosity, should have been. Though my eyes saw nothing, my heart felt the weight of hell staring back at me. Sitting on my butt a few feet from my open doorway, I wholly questioned my sanity. I blinked over and over again, waiting for them to show me the truth behind the veil of reality. Seconds passed and nothing happened.

A sigh began in my heavy lungs and made its way out through pursed lips. From the dark void of my porch, a screeching gust of foul air blasted my face with such force my clothes press against my skin. The smell was similar to rotten meat. Terrified as all the fucks in hell, I screamed back into the blast of air. Using my foot, I kicked the door closed, slamming it against the darkness. In an instant, I was on my knees, clinging to the doorknob. I flipped the deadbolt over and collapsed against the door. My heart pounding in my chest, all I could hear was the rush of blood in my ears. I sat for a moment, anticipating further contact.

Silence. I scrambled toward my bedroom half on all fours, half on my own two feet. Moving so quickly through the room, I slammed into my bedside table, knocking the things on top to the floor. Even in the darkened room, I saw the glint of my shiny, freshly cleaned, Beretta. I checked the clip, to be on the safe side, and flipped the safety off.

Eerie silence filled the small apartment. Atrophy was setting in, and my legs were beginning to protest any movement. Not believing for a minute the horror show was over, I found a spot to perch on the edge of the couch, facing the door, and waited.

I sat in the dark, shining pistol in hand, and waited for evil to bust down my door.

Bring it on, bitch.

A thud slammed against the door and I jumped. Another rocked the door against the frame. Another. And another. Until I thought, whatever beastly thing was on the other side, would bust right through.

I trained my gun on the center of the door. My heart thudded wildly in my chest, but I my hands remained steady. Whatever was trying to bust in my door wouldn't leave in one piece. I might not either.

"What in the fuck!" I screamed at the door when it burst open.

In the night that never seemed to end, the night that never gave way to the shiny light of day, fiction charged through and sunk its teeth into reality.

I am the gory mess it left behind. Me and my bigass gun.

Reality bites.

One.

The lonely traveler.

CPSIA information can be obtained
at www.ICGtesting.com
Printed in the USA
LVHW111629211022
731243LV00029B/1167/J

9 781735 863559